Wow, another book. Every time I'm done writing and have reread my story about 72 times, I have the same feeling. I'm excited, nervous, exhaling, sweaty, anxious, can't breathe, smiling ear to ear, second guessing, and ready for the world to read. I keep asking myself did I do everything I wanted to do with characters and scenes. I always think of something I should have added or something I should have changed. All in all, I'm always very pleased and look forward to feedback I get from readers. That is what keeps this pen moving.

When I wrote the first book about 12 years ago as I sat at work bored out of my mind, I never imagined I'd be right here, right now finishing up book #8(*Survivin' Tha Game* is 2 books in 1 ☺). Anywho, the feeling is surreal. I'm truly blessed.

As mentioned in *Devious Savages*, there are a lot of those Savage women and I know I introduced you to a gang of drama involving them all, and now I'm taking a few of them and telling their personal story. The Savage series isn't a sequel or trilogy and my goal is for all the books to stand alone. I don't want my readers feeling lost because they missed a book, but, of course, I'd like you to read them all ☺. These next few books are before the time of *Devious Savages* and after, and maybe when I'm done giving you more insight on characters I'll pen a *Devious Savages 2*.

Big thanks to Sheperd Photography for the picture and Ashley Paden for bringing Lexi Savage to life by being the model for the cover. Bigger thanks to all my readers. Good, bad, or ugly, you guys support me and that's priceless! Much love to my kids and grandkids, as always, they keep me motivated. Don't just follow your dreams, chase 'em down and catch 'em in a headlock!

Over and out ☺

Leila J

www.mytimepublications.com
www.facebook.com/leilajefferson
www.twitter.com/leilajefferson(haven't been on there much, but I'm gonna get back in twittermode soon)

SAVAGE
INSTINCT

By Leila Jefferson

Time Publications

www.mytimepublications.com

ISBN 13: 978-0-9830518-5-5

First Printing 2012

Library Congress Of Control Number: on file

Printed in United States of America

10 9 8 7 6 5 4 3 2 1

Also By Leila Jefferson

Survivin' Tha Game
He's A Keeper
Every Man's Dream
Scorned Hearts
Chronicles Of A Single Chick
Devious Savages

Anthologies

That's The Way Love Goes
Tasty Temptations
A Place To Go
Naughty & Definitely Not Nice

SAVAGE
INSTINCT

CHAPTER 1

"Lexi, go sit on ya Uncle Bank Roll lap and get ya dolla," Candy said to her daughter.

At twenty nine, Candy was gone beyond the point of return. She had been prostituting since she was eleven and her parents made her sit on laps when she was younger just as she did her girls. Her first lap sitting was at five, and she had done so much more before she ran away like her Yesina and hit the streets on her own. While sitting at the bus stop on Telegraph Street a guy picked up Candy and became her pimp. She raked in lots of money for him. She had known so much for her age and the men loved it. She got pregnant by one of her tricks when she was fifteen, who became her man, and had another baby by him a year and a half later.

Derrick was thirty one when he saw Candy walking down the street in cut off shorts and a half shirt. He knew she was a hoe and that was just what he needed. He had just gotten over the heartbreak of his woman having a baby by his brother and he never wanted to love again. He pulled over and picked her up, and her skills kept him going back for more. He didn't know how many tricks she had turned and he didn't know why he trusted her, but when she said she was pregnant he instantly knew the baby was his. Her pimp got rid of her, and she prostituted her pregnant body for food and room money.

Derrick showed up every now and again to fuck her, but he didn't want to take her in and take care of her for her to turn around and deceive him. When she finally had Yesina, he saw the

Savage genes all over her, only she was chocolate like her mother. A couple of years after Lexi was born, Derrick got tired of trying to chase Candy down to see about his kids or having his ex sister in law, Elizabeth, call him because the kids were over there, so he moved in her two bedroom, low income apartment in East Oakland. Besides, going to Elizabeth's was a constant reminder of the hurt when he saw the youngest daughter.

While Derrick robbed, Candy sold pussy when money was gone from her welfare check. Feeling frustrated from having two small babies, they both started getting high to take away from the stresses of their life and the girls were left to fend for themselves.

Candy's once chocolate skin looked dull and dry. Her five feet seven frame was once curvy with 38D tits and a round apple bottom. Over the years, her tits and ass became droopy, but at the end of the day her pussy and mouth still worked. That was all she needed to make a few dollars here and there. She used to have long, thick hair but cut it all off so she wouldn't have to worry about combing it, and she always wore too much makeup when she called herself going out to turn tricks.

Derrick looked old and dirty. His two front teeth were missing from being knocked out by a young drug dealer he tried to rob. In the end, it didn't matter to him because he still made out with forty dollars and five rocks. No one would have believed he was once a fine man that made over fifty thousand a year and lived in a plush house with a promising future. The infidelity from someone he thought was going to be his wife made him turn down a devastating path of destruction. There were times he couldn't look at himself in the mirror because he was so ashamed.

Lexi laid on the floor on her stomach looking at music videos. Yesina had paid for bootleg cable with money she had gotten from Bank Roll before she ran away. Lexi didn't know how long the cable would work, but she planned to watch videos until it was turned off or until her parents sold the TV. She loved looking at the half naked girls that the rappers rapped about. She wanted to be fly and fabulous just like them, and she vowed one day she would. She wanted the long weave, the perfect makeup, and a banging body. She practiced her dance moves in front of the

mirror, preparing herself for her big break. She turned her head toward the couch behind her and eyed Bank Roll.

Lexi stood up, smoothed out her dress, and as she walked toward him, Bank Roll smiled and let out a lust filled chuckle as she jumped on his lap. She sat sideways with her arms draped around his neck while she looked at him. Bank Roll was forty three, and looked great for a man of his age since he had never done any hard labor and always had money. He was light skinned with wavy hair and stood five feet eight, although his presence made him seem to be well over six feet. He had a thing for the young girls and had no problem fulfilling his wishes since he had money to throw away. He loved the fact that two of the biggest fiends had the prettiest little chocolate girls. Lexi sat on Bank Roll's lap plenty of times before, but since Yesina was gone she wondered would it be the time she had been waiting for.

"Give me my dolla first," Lexi said in a sassy tone with her hand out.

"That's right, baby, get ya money first," Candy rooted before leaving the living room to go to the kitchen for her high.

Bank Roll went in his pocket and gave Lexi a dollar. She looked at it as if she were trying to make sure it wasn't fake, and once satisfied that it wasn't she tucked it in her young cleavage as she had seen her mother do many times before since her dress didn't have pockets.

"Ya momma and daddy owe me some money, but I said we can let all that go if you sit on my lap for a little while." Lexi shrugged her shoulders like it made no difference to her one way or the other. "You miss your sister?" he asked as he patted her back.

"Yea, I don't have nobody to play with since she ran away," Lexi said sadly as she looked toward the floor.

Bank Roll rubbed her arm. "I miss her, too. I don't have anybody to play with, either. Can we play together?"

Lexi gave him a big smile. She was a grown woman in a little girl's body, and Bank Roll was about to find out she knew exactly what she was doing. "Do you like to play jacks or hopscotch?" she asked innocently as she laid her head on his shoulder.

It was her time. She felt the excitement build inside of her. What Bank Roll didn't know was that Lexi knew full well what was going on. She had watched her mother fuck tricks over the years. She watched her dad with his head between her legs and was intrigued at how her mother moaned. She had watched Bank Roll fuck Yesina, and she watched Yesina and a few of the hood boys fuck plenty of times.

She saw Yesina put many dicks in her mouth and heard how the boys moaned, including Bank Roll. They would put their head between Yesina's legs and she'd moan and yell for them to, 'keep licking there.' They would get on top of her and open her legs as wide as they could before they plunged inside of her. They would fuck all night, and Lexi would lie on the floor and play with her bud, wanting to feel like she imagined her sister felt.

Yesina loved fucking. When Bank Roll first had her sit on his lap she wasn't sure what was going on, but he played with her bud and made her tingle, and she liked it. He kept doing that and then began sticking his fingers inside of her, which felt even better. When he stuck his dick inside of her, she went wild. He had opened the flood gates and she wanted to fuck all the time. She just didn't want to fuck Bank Roll. He was old, and she wanted the young dope boys that she saw on the corners. She let anybody fuck her that wanted it. She was an inferno, and when Bank Roll found out she was giving it to anybody free he told her she had to stop or he would have to punish her. She ran away a few days later.

"Undo my pants and pull it out." Lexi did as told and freed his dick. It was hard and smooth. Bank Roll put his hands on top of Lexi's and moved it up and down his shaft. He moaned. "That feels real good. Can Bank Roll make you feel good?"

"Yes."

"Keep doing what you're doing." He removed his hands from Lexi's, slid her panties to the side, and gently rubbed her lips that felt like peach fuzz. "You like that?"

"Mmm hmm," Lexi moaned. Yesina was right. It felt good when she touched herself, but it felt better having Bank Roll touch her.

She watched the late night movies on cable and had stolen an X rated tape from her cousin, Chrisette, and watched it over and

Taste me," she demanded as she held her pussy lips open like a grown woman while looking him in the eyes. There was no way she was going to let him go without experiencing what it felt like to have someone licking her bud.

Bank Roll raised a brow and got aroused all over again. "I like a bitch that know what she need." He leaned down and buried his face between her legs. He had already tasted her sweet juices from his finger and wanted to taste her directly, but wasn't sure she was ready to go that far.

Yesina was right, having a tongue lick her felt better than she could have ever imagined. Lexi wrapped her legs around Bank Roll's neck as she rotated her hips. Her eyes rolled in the back of her head as the sensation gave her a feeling she hoped would never end. She felt tingles and tried to think of something else to keep that monster feeling from coming that always drained her. Not able to hold on much longer, she finally whispered, "Right there, daddy. Lick that pussy good," just as she had heard Yesina say many times before. Bank Roll sucked and licked until her young body convulsed wildly. His dick was so hard he knew it was going to explode. He wanted to slide between her chocolate thighs, but he knew she definitely wasn't ready for that. Lexi sat up and kissed his lips so softly. An outsider would have looked at the scene as disgusting and mind boggling, but to people who lived life as Bank Roll and Lexi had, it was the norm.

He went in his pocket and gave her another fifty. "You gonna be Bank Roll special bitch. I got plans for you." She got up and went to the bathroom while Bank Roll fixed his clothes and walked to the kitchen. "Fuck! That lil' bitch a thoroughbred up in there. I ain't never came so fuckin' hard. Y'all been training her ass?" Bank Roll asked Derrick and Candy.

They both sat at the table with wide eyes. "She good to clear shit?" Candy said, her words jumbled together.

"Y'all niggas can get high anytime ya want if I can have her." Bank Roll tipped his hat and walked out the door.

Lexi felt excited. She went to the bathroom but remembered the soap was in the kitchen because she had to use it to wash dishes, so she stopped on the other side of the wall to hear what Bank Roll said about her. She knew her parents loved to get

Leila Jefferson

high, so she would have Bank Roll making her feel good all the time. She didn't know why Yesina ran away. She could get fucked by Bank Roll, get money, and she could fuck all the hood boys, too.

She finally went to the kitchen to get the soap. "Supa star," Candy said when she saw Lexi's sperm covered dress.

Derrick sat up and looked at her. He firmly gripped her upper arms and stood her directly in front of him. "Lemme tell you something. As long as you got a hot pussy, you bet not neva be broke. Niggas pay top dollar for good pussy, so you need to make sure Bank Roll give you way more than he did the next time. Your pussy may feel good from what a nigga do to you, but best believe he feelin' way better." Lexi almost told him about the hundred dollars, but she knew they would want her money. She simply nodded her head. "Don't fuck with these drugs because that shit fuck off your worth. You a Savage and you better use them Savage instincts at all times. Pussy is power, and pussy rule the muthafuckin' world." He looked at Candy. "You hear that shit? We can get high anytime we want. Let's go, bitch."

Candy jumped up from the table and followed behind Derrick wearing baggy sweats, pumps, and a house robe with no shirt or bra underneath.

Lexi stood there as she watched them leave, knowing they wouldn't be back for a while. The words her father said were etched in her mind. Bank Roll had just given her one hundred and one dollars just for her to rub his dick, and let him rub her bud and lick it. She hadn't sucked his dick or have it inside of her pussy. She wondered how much she would get when she did more.

Lexi got the soap from the kitchen sink and went to take a shower. "Niggas ain't ready for what's about to hit them," she said as she cleansed herself. At eleven years old, Lexi was in the makings of becoming a beast that plenty weren't ready for.

CHAPTER 2

"I wanna feel you inside of me," Lexi begged as she lowered her eyes and gave Bank Roll the look that drove him wild.

It was hard, literally, but Bank Roll gave Lexi a stern look. "Lookie here, don't neva beg no nigga for no dick. Dick is a dime a dozen, baby girl. You make that nigga beg, plead, throw money at your ass just for a whiff of that sweet pussy. Best believe you gonna feel me. I'm gonna bust that cherry 'cause that's my cherry, but it's gonna be on my time."

Lexi looked down at the floor. "Sorry," she whispered.

He put his finger under her chin and lifted her head. "Look at me," Bank Roll said evenly. "Don't apologize for shit you do, and don't let a nigga make you look at the floor. Always keep ya head up. Your confidence is yours, don't let nobody take that."

Bank Roll had showed her everything. He taught her how to kiss a nigga so good he would cum. He licked her pussy and ass, made her scream his name, and then taught her to act like the nut that overtook her body meant nothing. He taught her how to suck dick and deep throat like a certified pro. He told her that was gonna be her money maker because niggas were fools for an unforgettable head job and loved when a bitch could take every inch of him in her mouth. She sucked his balls and licked his ass as he fingered her tight hole. She was like a sponge and soaked up everything he taught her. He wanted to desensitize her from the nuts she busted because that would keep her head on straight, unlike her sister.

Yesina was just as young and hot, but she let the chase of a nut take over. Instead of doing what Bank Roll tried to breed her for, she wanted to give the pussy away for free to any lil' nigga that wanted it. Last Bank Roll heard, she was in LA somewhere fucking with a nigga that was beating her ass. She could have been living in luxury with everyone envious of her, but she wanted to stay in the streets like a bum so there was nothing Bank Roll could do.

He knew Lexi was different. Even though he took care of her and bought clothes, shoes, got her hair and nails done, and kept her pockets together, she still had her hand out whenever she knew he wanted her to make him feel good. *You gotta pay to play* had been the motto he made her live by. She was smart, so he made sure she went to school and kept her grades up. He knew in life she needed book smarts as well as street smarts. He wanted her to be well rounded. He held back from lying up with her every day like he wanted. Her pussy was always so hot and wet and it begged for him to play with it, but he had to practice what he preached and not get caught up.

Besides, Bank Roll had plenty of arm candy. He had a dozen women that were at his every beck and call. He loved the way Lexi never showed an ounce of jealousy. She kissed him when he left and was always ready for him whenever he got in the house. She treated his women like family and gave them the utmost respect.

"You going to be thirteen in a week. What you want for your birthday?" Bank Roll asked Lexi as she sat on his lap and grinded her hot box on him.

Lexi almost said she wanted him, but she knew that was the wrong answer. "Diamonds and cash, daddy."

Bank Roll smacked her ass. "That's my bitch. You been practicing on that pole?"

"Sure have."

"Go put on something sexy and show me what you workin' with."

Lexi got up and slowly walked to the room. She sashayed her ass and right before she disappeared through the doorway, she turned around and blew him a kiss. She moved in with Bank Roll

three months earlier when her parents died. One of the dope dealers kicked in the door to her old apartment, and killed Derrick and Candy for stealing from him. Word on the street was Candy offered to suck the dude's dick for a rock and when he had his pants down and about to bust, Derrick crept behind him and hit him in the head. They took all his rocks and money, and when he came to he went right over there and shot both of them in the face with no remorse.

Lexi had just gotten home from having dinner with Bank Roll. He wanted her to get in the house early because she had school the next day. She heard when the door was kicked in and heard the yelling and cussing, but she stayed in her room and didn't utter a sound. When she heard the gunshots, she prayed they wouldn't kill her as well. When she heard the tires burning rubber on the street outside, she exhaled. She slowly walked to the living room and saw what she had feared. Her parents lay there in a bloody mess. The sight was somewhat of a relief to her. There was a bit of sadness because she no longer had parents, but there was more happy because she knew her life was about to change. It was her fate.

Yesina showed her face for a couple of days after they died to gather the belongings she had left behind. She seemed to be mad when she saw Lexi because she had on diamonds and gold with designer labels. She looked like a boss bitch. Yesina, on the other hand, had gone from dope boy to dope boy since she had ran away, sucking and fucking until she met Goose, who had taken her to Vegas with him to pimp her out. Goose had been in jail with Devon, who always talked about Yesina Savage and how freaky she was, that she knew how to work it. When Goose got out he had one mission in mind.

Yesina was in love and did what he wanted. She never saw it coming when he start hooking her up with niggas, saying bills needed to be paid. She wanted to be down and do whatever her man needed. She went from being hooked up to niggas Goose brought around to standing on corners or setting niggas up. When things didn't go right or the money wasn't enough from a set up, Goose took it out on Yesina with his fists.

After having a fight with him, she called her girl, Bianca, and to cry to her, and Bianca was the one who told her about her parents. Goose said he would take her home for the funeral, but she would need to work double time to make up for the money lost. Soon after the funeral, they headed to Reno so she could work her magic there. He wasn't nearly as generous as Bank Roll and there were no special gifts or surprises, only black eyes and bruises. She hated Lexi for living the life she should have been living.

Lexi emerged from the room in a green G-string and matching bra with clear stripper heels. She walked toward the pole that was in the middle of the living room and grabbed it. Bank Roll turned on the music and Lexi began to dance. She climbed the pole and swung her body around it. She did all kinds of tricks that Bank Roll approved of. He knew stripping was something she could always do if he wasn't around and she needed extra cash. She let her bra fall and her perky mounds called his name. He unzipped his pants and began stroking himself as he looked at his young bitch. She seemed to never break eye contact as she teased him with her body. The long, curly weave she wore was wild and messy, adding to her sex appeal. She removed her G-string and tossed it at Bank Roll. He sniffed it as he rubbed the panties over his face. Bank Roll tossed twenty dollar bills at her the entire time she danced. She climbed to the top again and slid down to the floor in a split. Then, she crawled over toward him. When she approached the couch he sat on, she took his hand from his dick and began licking and slurping on it. Bank Roll laid his head back on the couch.

She is way before her time.

Lexi, always making sure she got hers, crawled up on Bank Roll's body and got in a 69 position so that he could taste her juices as she continued to suck his dick. As she came, she took his length in her mouth and sucked as hard as she could until his juices began spurting down her throat. She opened her legs wider as he lapped up all of her juices. She had to be still for a moment to let the feeling subside. Once she calmed down, she twisted her body off of Bank Roll's and raised a brow as she stretched out her garter.

Bank Roll laughed. "Next time, do that before you start slurping on my dick." He put ten one hundred dollar bills in her garter before she turned and walked to the room.

"Wake up, baby girl. Somebody's officially a woman today," Bank Roll said as he walked in Lexi's room. She wanted to sleep with him in his bed, but it was too much temptation for Bank Roll and what he tried to do. He got her situated in the second room, and she always slept naked in case he wanted to come in during the middle of the night or early in the morning to taste her pussy.

Lexi woke up and stretched her chocolate body. Her B cups had grown another cup, and she had grown woman curves. Her peach fuzz had grown into a little bush that Bank Roll requested she keep neatly shaved. Her lips were full and soft, and she was beginning to be fully aware of what she possessed as a woman.

"Good morning, daddy," Lexi said seductively. She got on her knees and kissed his lips sweetly as she did every morning. She batted her long, false eyelashes at him as she rubbed his arm through his silk pajamas.

Bank Roll pulled a box from behind his back. Lexi smiled as she grabbed it from him with excitement. She opened it to see a diamond necklace, tennis bracelet, and earrings. Bank Roll had intended to wait until later that night after he took her out, but he couldn't help himself. He pulled Lexi closer to him and kissed her. She sucked his tongue and swirled hers around his mouth just as he had taught her. Instinctively, she reached down and felt the bulge in his pants. She slowly unbuttoned his shirt and kissed down his chest, making her way to his dick.

Bank Roll stopped her. "No, it's your birthday. Daddy gonna make you feel real good." He smiled as he took off his pajamas and looked at his prized possession.

Without being told, Lexi lay back on her bed and opened her legs. Getting her pussy licked always made her feel good. Bank Roll licked and sucked while he fingered her pussy. He put in two, and then three. Before long, he had all four fingers in her sloshing wet pussy while stimulating her clit with his tongue. She moaned

and grinded beneath him, and she loved the way he made her feel. "Yes, daddy, eat that pussy," she moaned. "Mmm, suck that clit."

After Lexi came, Bank Roll stood up as he watched her play with her pussy and look at him with hypnotizing, dark eyes. He went in the jar on her dresser that was filled with condoms and retrieved one. "Never let a nigga fuck you raw," was all he said before he began slowly working himself inside of her. He wanted to hit it without the condom, but he had to make sure she learned to trick the right way. She moaned and gyrated, excited to finally feel him penetrate her. She clenched her pussy muscles like he had taught her. "Not yet, baby girl, let me get inside all the way first," Bank Roll whispered. She circled her clit as he sank deeper and deeper. Finally, his entire length was inside of her and it was the best feeling she had ever felt. He penetrated her walls as he slowly moved in and out of her. Getting in the groove, she began to tighten her muscles around his dick. "Shit, baby girl, you gonna make daddy nut. You doing real good, but relax a little so we both can enjoy this for as long as possible."

Lexi played with her nipples as she looked up at Bank Roll. She wanted to feel him inside of her all day, so although she wanted to pop her pussy all over his dick and make him scream her name, she slowed her gyrating and stopped clenching her pussy muscles. He had been her everything since that first mind blowing experience in her parents' living room and he never steered her wrong.

As Bank Roll picked her up and laid on the bed so she could ride him, she wondered how her sister could be so stupid and let a nigga hit her. When Yesina showed up for their parents' funeral she looked so worn down. She wondered where she was and how she was doing. Finally, Lexi pushed thoughts of her sister out of her head and enjoyed her daddy. She knew she would never be like her sister. She was going to feel good and get paid. She knew her position and she knew Bank Roll was getting her ready to fuck other niggas. She'd fuck anybody for him and turn them out to keep them coming back for more. She was going to make Bank Roll prouder than any other bitch ever had.

14

She began bouncing on his dick wildly and he knew he had to take control. He turned her over once more and positioned himself on top of her again.

"Fuck this pussy, daddy. Fuck me harder," Lexi begged. She winded her hips and bucked wildly against him. She knew he wanted her to slow down, but the feeling was too good. The dick had her gone. The curve in his dick hit a spot she hadn't been aware of before. He felt the sensation take over her.

"Daddy hitting that G spot," he whispered to her. "If you get a nigga that hit this spot right here," he slowed his pace and went deeper, "then that nigga can damn near own you. Unless," he paused and stroked her a few times, "you can own your G spot," Bank Roll said slowly. That shit felt so good, Lexi almost didn't pay attention to what was being said. "Calm down, baby girl. Take over this dick and own that sexy ass G spot. Use me to get your nut."

Lexi took a deep breath. *Mind over matter, bitch*, she told herself. She concentrated, but nothing could prepare her for what she felt. Bank Roll held her legs wide open as he hit her spot continuously. She came all over his dick, coating the condom with her juices.

"Did that feel good to you?" he asked as he slowed his stroke to let her catch her breath.

"Yes," she confessed as she breathed heavily. It felt like her whole body had been stuck by a million tiny pins, but it was a good feeling. Her toes curled so hard she thought they would break. When she closed her eyes, she saw spots. Bank Roll had made her feel so good many times before, but what he just did to her was better than anything he had done before. She could easily see why her sister wanted to fuck all the time. She concluded that the orgasm she had must have been what crackheads felt like when they got high.

"Here comes another one." He picked up the pace, making her cum again while she was still in her thoughts. "That's right, give me all them juices." Lexi tried to hold back, but she kept cumming and cumming. Finally, Bank Roll let go of his own load. "I'm gonna let you slide because it's your birthday and it's the first time you felt some dick in ya, but get that shit under control."

Bank Roll quietly put on his clothes as Lexi tried to gain her senses.

That night, Lexi moved in Bank Roll's room.

CHAPTER 3

"I got to run out of town for about a week to handle business. Bianca gonna come chill with you while I'm gone."

Lexi gave Bank Roll a kiss as she hugged him tightly. "OK, daddy." She looked at Bianca. "Hey, girl."

"Look at you, all grown and shit. You look just like your sister."

"I hear that all the time. I wish she was here, we would be runnin' this shit."

Lexi wasn't exactly sure she'd run anything. She was ready to do what Bank Roll had been training her for, but he hadn't sent her with anyone. She heard niggas inquire about her and Bank Roll always told them she wasn't ready yet. She started to get worried because she began to think she hadn't been learning fast enough or the right way, but when she heard Bank Roll check a nigga about checking for her too hard, instincts told her it was something different. She was prepared to turn as many tricks Bank Roll wanted her to, but she loved the fact that he wanted her all to himself.

"You got that right. Damn, she let the dick rule her." Bianca looked around to make sure Bank Roll was out of earshot. "But, I see you hella ruling that dick, bitch." She gave Lexi a hi-five and smiled.

"I learned from the best," Lexi admitted. "Where your kids?"

"BJ with my momma and Shaquanisha at my sister house."

"Oh, OK."

Bianca had just turned twenty and was one of the girls Bank Roll sent on dates. Her kids were three and one. BJ was by a local dope boy and Shaquanisha could have been anyone's child. She didn't care either way because the money she made allowed her to give her mother and sister more than enough money to care for her kids. She had things to do and she didn't have time to take care of babies.

Bank Roll walked into the room with a small suitcase. "Take care of my baby girl." He gave Bianca a kiss, and then turned to Lexi. "I'll see you in a few, baby girl." He gave her a deeper kiss, the kiss of a lover that would be missing his significant other while gone on a business trip.

"Damn, girl, what you do to that nigga?" Bianca inquired. "I never seen him kissing no bitches like that." She envied Lexi. She wasn't in love with Bank Roll or wanted to be with him, she envied the fact that Lexi had someone that adored her and took care of her. Bianca knew if Lexi was old enough he would have probably married her. He never said it, but everyone knew he loved her.

"He taught me everything. I know he's always got my back, and till I take my last breath I'll always have his."

Bianca looked at the young girl and saw something she had never seen before in her lifetime. "Damn, you're in love."

"Fuck yea, I am. I won't deny that shit ever. I love Bank Roll. That's my nigga to the end. And, any bitch or nigga that try to come between that, well, they'll get some shit they ain't looking for."

"Damn, Lex, for you to be so young you a real ass bitch. I can respect that shit 'cause you the first one to get that nigga heart, and I'm glad 'cause you deserve it."

"Do you ever get fucked up that he don't love you like that?" Lexi asked.

"Girl, I got hella for Bank Roll. He took me in and showed me shit I wouldn't have learned anywhere else, and at the end of the day I want him to be happy. You make him happy. How can I be mad at that?" She shrugged her shoulders.

"You a real bitch, too, Bianca."

"You smoke?"

"I have a couple of times."

"Well, we 'bout to smoke tonight." Bianca went in her Douney & Bourke purse, and pulled out a twenty sack and a blunt. She split the blunt expertly and put the green, broken up buds inside. After she took a toke, she passed it to Lexi. "If you not a G, don't try to hit it too hard. Take a small puff and pass that shit, bitch."

Lexi felt like she was being challenged. She had mastered dick and there was no way she wasn't going to master some punk ass weed. "Bitch, I got this." Lexi took a long toke and held the smoke inside a long as she could. When it seemed as if her whole body was engulfed in smoke, she finally let out a small puff. She hit it once more before she passed it back to Bianca.

"Damn, vacuum lungs. OK."

Bianca rolled another blunt once the first one was finished. They sat there looking Chinese in the eyes because they were so low.

"Bianca, I love Bank Roll, but I don't want to be that bitch he don't want me to be. Nothing is supposed to matter and I'm not allowed to have feelings. It's hard not to tell him I love him. I don't have friends, and I hope you can be one. If I seem too caught up, check me."

Bianca waved her off. "Girl, you straight."

"No, B, I'm serious. I need a bitch in my corner for real. A real bitch that ain't trying to get over or set me up."

"I'm old school, so we gonna pinky swear right here." She held her pinky out so Lexi could wrap her pinky around it. "Long as you stay as real as you are right now, I got your muthafuckin' back. Let's be real, though. Who been here since you moved in?"

Lexi shrugged her shoulders. "Nobody really."

"Bank Roll got bitches that love his dirty draws and they would be laid up. That should tell you something if nobody been laid up since you moved in."

"Damn, I guess you right. But, I still want you to keep me in check. I don't wanna set myself up for the okie doke."

Bianca looked at Lexi sideways. "That's so cute you can see how much he love you, but again, I got your back girl."

They hugged and that simple gesture started a bond that could never be broken.

***

Bank Roll returned from Vegas four days later. He came bearing gifts, bringing Lexi a Versace dress with matching shoes and a diamond ring that anyone would have sworn was an engagement ring. For Bianca, he had a designer dress and shoes as well with a gold necklace that had a diamond pendant. He also bought gifts for her kids. Bianca thanked him, and left him and Lexi to be alone.

"I missed you, daddy," she whispered in his ear as she sat on his lap.

"Daddy missed you, too," Bank Roll admitted. "Get dressed, we going to dinner."

Lexi jumped up and prepared herself for dinner. She took her time showering, washing every crevice of her curvaceous body. Bank Roll always told her it was important to make sure she stayed clean. She took long bubble baths every night and showered every morning. Even when her and Bank Roll messed around, she took a shower soon after to make sure she stayed fresh.

When she was done, she slowly lotioned herself as she waited for the curling iron to get hot. She added a few curls to her hair, and sprayed the Chanel No. 5 on her dress, wrists, and neck. It was Bank Roll's favorite scent. Their destination was The Cliff House in San Francisco. Lexi loved when Bank Roll took her out for five star dining in fancy restaurants where adults were the only patrons. She even loved when he ordered her meals for her, taking care of her like a real daddy was supposed to. She felt so grown up as she placed the linen napkin in her lap, sipped wine, compliments of the fake ID, and talked to her man while they waited for the food.

Bank Roll had her visit Mabel, one of the older women on his team. She was very refined and proper, and she taught Bank Roll's girls how to act, speak, and interact with others. Mabel's mother had taught etiquette classes back in the day so she knew everything about being a proper young lady.

"I missed you while you were gone, daddy." She looked at Bank Roll in his jazzy black suit with a gray shirt, and black and

gray striped tie. He could have easily been someone's business man that worked a nine to five.

Bank Roll smiled. "You told me that already, baby girl."

"I just want to make sure you know how much I missed you."

"I do." She beamed at him as her eyes sparkled.

Bank Roll looked at Lexi and was proud of himself. He had trained her to be better than any hoe he'd had, and he had plenty over the years. There was one problem, he had broken his number one rule and fell in love with her. She was so sweet and innocent, but so dangerous. She did any and everything for him, and did it with no questions. She had willingly given herself to him, and he wanted to keep her. When the waiter returned with their food, he watched as she smiled and thanked him. She was so poised. She could easily pass for a woman in her young twenties. She waited for Bank Roll to take his first bite before she began eating her own meal.

"Guess what?"

"What's up, baby girl?"

"I passed my finals. You're looking at an official high schooler now."

"That's my baby girl." Bank Roll smiled. He was proud. She was only thirteen, but had gotten skipped up a grade. He wanted her to keep those book smarts, and that was why he decided he wasn't going to lead her down the same path as he had led so many lost souls in the past. "You going to go to college and make a better life for yourself."

Lexi's eyes got big. She didn't know anyone that had gone to college. "College? You think I could go to college?"

"You gotta have an education in this life, baby girl. Streets smarts will get you a few places here and there, but book smarts will take you places you never been. You need both of those to be the total package. I already got your college fund put aside for you."

When Bank Roll said things like that, Lexi was determined to remain a straight A student. School was easy to her, and she liked going there to learn. She wanted to be everything he thought she should be. When he told her he grew up in Mississippi and

hadn't gone to school past the sixth grade because he had to work, she was determined to learn all the things he seemed to wish he had learned.

She wanted to show him she could be the best. She wanted to be well rounded and be the baddest bitch Bank Roll ever had. She listened intently as he shared one of his stories for what was probably the thousandth time.

"I was just about your age when I first came here to Cali. Uncle Willie taught me to play pool and we'd run game night after night. I ran numbers for Uncle Po and watched my big brother, Pootie, run his women. My granddaddy had a juke joint down south where everyone went to hustle some way or another and have fun. We come from a long line of hustlers. I watched them all and studied each of their crafts. I loved the way my brother had women selling their bodies with only sweet words and empty promises. Those bitches would do anything he said, they worshipped the ground he walked on. I learned finesse from him. Of course, when I got here I dabbled here and there, and found my way when I got my first bottom bitch. A few years later, I started getting some of this drug money."

"You're so smart."

"I got street smarts, but you gonna be a shining star. You got that potential, baby girl. I'm going to be so proud to see you walk across that stage when you graduate high school."

"I'll graduate top of my class, daddy. You just watch and see."

"I know you will. We gonna go somewhere special when you do." Bank Roll knew she would have been the most loyal bottom bitch he ever had, but he had bigger plans for her.

"I'm so lucky to have you. I'm gonna go above and beyond what you need from me." Lexi's eyes sparkled.

"You remind me so much of Betty Sue," Bank Roll said in almost a whisper.

"Who is she?" Lexi couldn't recall hearing the name before.

He sighed heavily. He removed his wallet from his pocket and took out a worn, black and white picture. He handed it to Lexi. She studied the beautiful, chocolate woman in the picture. Her

smile was so wide and bright. Her hair was long and straight. She had her arm around a much younger Bank Roll's neck, and he looked so happy. Lexi felt a small twinge of jealousy rise in her. Of all the women she had ever seen swoon over Bank Roll, the woman in the picture seemed more threatening than all of them.

"She was the first, and only, woman to break old Bank Roll's heart. That was a tough lesson for me, but I needed it and I'm glad I got it out of the way early."

Bank Roll had a faraway look in his eyes. He met Betty Sue almost a year after he had touched down in Oakland. They were at a bar celebrating his fourteenth birthday and he felt like the man. When he heard her order a drink, he knew she was from down south. Bank Roll drank with his uncles and brother like he was a grown man. When they saw him checking her out, they dared him to go talk to her. He smoothly walked over to the beauty at the bar and asked her name. They talked and he learned she was from Tennessee. She had had stopped in Oakland to visit her sister before she headed to Los Angeles to be a star. She wanted to be on the big screen and everybody back home told her she had the looks to make it. By the end of the night, Bank Roll had Betty Sue in his bed fucking her like a wild animal.

Pussy was nothing for him, he had been fucking with his brother's hoes since he was nine. They sucked his dick and fucked him like a grown man, so by the time he got to Betty Sue she couldn't tell he was still a boy.

He fell in love with Betty Sue. Her sweet smile and soft voice had him hooked. He hustled so he could lavish her with gifts and money, and she never saw the bright lights of LA. A couple months after she was supposed to officially be his woman, he found out she was fucking everyone, including his uncles and brother. Bank Roll was heartbroken, but Pootie pulled him to the side.

"Ain't none of these bitches worth shit. They pretty and can make you feel good, but at the end of the day they always looking at the nigga with the biggest dick or the biggest wallet. Don't ever get caught up thinking they ain't nothing but pussy."

"She said she loved me, bro."

"Lil' nigga, you a kid. I know you got a lil' game and think you the shit, but you still a kid."

"She said she wasn't trippin'."

Betty Sue was only nineteen herself and knew he was younger, but she figured he was maybe seventeen, eighteen. When she found out he was fourteen and still handled business like he did, she didn't care. Age didn't discriminate against the furs, fancy cars, and diamonds. She stood by her man proudly.

Pootie had stopped by their spot to holla at Bank Roll, but he wasn't there. Betty Sue invited him in and told him he could wait. When she flashed that bright smile and sashayed away from the front door, Pootie knew exactly what she wanted. He told Barbara, one of his hoes, to go wait for him in the car while he fucked the daylights out of Betty Sue. He gave her a few dollars because she had some good pussy and told her to give him a ring when she wanted more.

They started fucking, and it wasn't long before she was letting Po, Willie, and anybody else Pootie sent her way get a piece of her goods. Bank Roll was so hard on his hustle he hadn't noticed until one night after he handled some business he stopped by his brother's place. He walked in and heard sounds of fucking, but that was nothing new. When he walked to the back and saw his Betty Sue sucking Willie's dick while Po fucked her from behind, he was devastated.

"That's 'cause you was buying her all that shit and treating her good. Treat all these bitches like shit and it'll get you further. Now, that Betty got some good pussy and she a looker, put that bitch on the track." Pootie tapped his brother on the back. "Go get yourself a drink and get that love shit out ya system."

Bank Roll did just that. He got a fifth of Gin and got pissy drunk, but he couldn't pimp out the woman he loved. He did, however, let Pootie handle his business. Before anyone knew it, Betty Sue had become one of his best bitches on the streets. Bank Roll kept that picture to remind him love wasn't shit.

CHAPTER 4

It was three years after Lexi first sat on Bank Roll's lap and he told her she was going to be his special bitch because she made him cum so hard. She was no longer a little girl. In her eyes, she was a grown ass woman. She sat on the front porch of immaculate house she lived in and waited for her ride to the funeral home. Bank Roll had been everything she had ever wanted. He introduced her to everything sexually, even anal. By the time he was finished, she was a top notch bitch. She knew how to talk, how to walk, how to act, and how to get paid. She made good grades in school and was destined to be a lawyer or doctor or business mogul. All the niggas in the hood wanted her so bad they could taste it, but they knew she was off limits. There was a silent celebration for Bank Roll's demise because Lexi Savage had become fair game.

"Come jump in the ride," Devin said to Lexi.

"What's up, Devin?" she asked as she slid in the passenger seat of Acura Legend like a panther.

"Damn, chocolate, you done grew up," Devin said as he looked her up and down. "Your sister been around?"

"She ain't been around since my folks died. She in LA or Vegas or somewhere turning tricks for a nigga that whoop her ass," Lexi said like it disgusted her.

"Is that right?"

"Yea. She don't look the same. I hope that bitch wake up. She ain't using her power the right way."

Devin licked his lips. "So, how good was Bank Roll at showing you the ropes? You know I was s'posed to get some of you when I got out of Rita, then this shit happened."

Lexi smirked. She knew nobody was promised shit of hers, but she played along. Lexi leaned over and whispered in his ear, "I'm not in the Boy Scouts, daddy, so I don't know what ropes you talking about."

Devin laughed. "Did he stretch that pussy open like he did Yesina? I bet you remember all them nights I fucked your sister. I used to see you lying on the floor finger popping that pussy."

Lexi stroked his dick while she sucked on his earlobe. "He taught me a lot, daddy. You wanna see what I learned?" Her soft, enticing voice was like silk.

"You gonna make me fuckin' wrap my car," Devin said when a horn blew from him swerving in the next lane.

Lexi leaned back in her seat and laughed. Devin had always been fine to her. He was dark skinned with neat corn rolls. His front teeth were gold and his jewels were right. He wasn't too flashy, but the chain and ring with the diamonds in his ear let people know he had a little paper.

"How much is this worth to you?" She pulled her skirt up and exposed her pink middle that lay between those chocolate lips. Devin swerved again. "Oops, keep ya eyes on the road, daddy." Lexi leaned back and played with her pussy while she moaned. She didn't stop until she came, which was right when they reached CP Bannon Funeral Home. She put her finger in Devin's mouth and he licked away her juices. "Thanks for the ride." Lexi shot him a sly smile as she slid out of the car.

Devin sat in his car as he waited for his erection to go down. "I gotta have that bitch," he said under his breath before he got out of the car to go in the funeral home and pay his last respects.

Lexi slowly walked in the funeral home and all eyes were on her. She was envied by many because she had accomplished what many before her had tried. Lexi's five feet six frame seemed to float toward the casket, making everyone stop what they were doing and stare at her. The black dress she wore clung to her curves. The black stilettos gave her legs a sexy shape. The shades

she wore covered half of her face, almost giving her a mysterious aura. As she walked to the front of the funeral home, her hips did a slow, seductive sway. She walked to Bank Roll's white and gold casket, and placed a red rose on his lifeless body. She held her weave back as she kissed him on the lips, leaving her red lipstick as evidence that she had been there. She turned, knowing all eyes were still on her, walked back down the aisle, and exited as quickly as she arrived.

"I'm glad that old ass pervert finally kicked the bucket," Yesina said.

"Bitch, when you get in town?" Lexi smiled and hugged her sister tightly.

"I knew you would be here."

"Yea, he an old pervert, but I had a lot of love for that nigga," Lexi said as she looked back at the funeral home once more. She tried to hold back the tears because she knew Bank Roll wouldn't want her to cry, but she could literally feel her heart breaking. She didn't know what she was going to do.

"I hella wanna go in there and spit on that nigga."

"Don't hate the player, hate the game, sister. That nigga gave me a gang of knowledge. Love it or hate it, but momma and daddy the one that sold your ass to him to get high. He did what any nigga would do with a young bitch presented to them for payment. I thought you liked that shit, anyways?"

"Bitch, sound like *your* nasty ass liked that shit, taking up for that nigga."

Lexi lifted her shades and looked Yesina in the eyes. "I did."

Yesina laughed as she shook her head. "Bitch, get in." Lexi hopped in the Mustang convertible with her sister and they let the wind lead them.

"Whose is this?"

"Todd. That's my new nigga," Yesina explained.

"Oh, so what's new? You looking good." Lexi was clearly lying. Yesina had what looked to be a fresh black eye and her lip was swollen.

"Me and Todd heading to ATL to make some money, get over on a few niggas. I see the way you looking at my eye. Yea,

me and that nigga be scrapping, but best believe I give it just as hard as I get it."

Lexi shook her head as she looked at her sister. "Why you even wanna deal with some shit like that? What gives a nigga the right to hit on you?"

Yesina laughed. "We fuck and make up. I love him and he loves me. I don't care how many bitches I gotta fight, I'm keeping mine." Her smile instantly faded. "You need to meet him. Come to Sue house with me, that's his momma."

"How you meet him?"

"I was out and about with that nigga Goose I was with when I came around when mom and dad died. He was wilding out on me, and Todd stepped in and served that nigga. Been with him since."

"So, you left a nigga that hit you for another nigga that hit you?"

Yesina ignored Lexi. "So, where you gonna stay at now?"

Lexi didn't push. She leaned back in the seat and thought for a minute. "I'll probably go see what's up with Auntie Liz and the crew. I need a change of pace. I need to slow down. Bank Roll was giving me money I stacked, plus, I got some gems in my possession that will keep me paid forever."

"Man, remember all those bus rides we took over there when momma and daddy would be gone for days? She never asked questions, just let us in, gave us some fresh clothes, and fed us."

"I know. Then, momma ass would come over acting a fool, acting like she kidnapped us or something. Auntie Liz would give us a grocery bag full of food, backpack full of clean clothes, and let us leave."

"Yea, she always been top notch. Uncle Chris died, but they still got a good life."

"Why we had to have the fucked up parents?"

"Lexi, we're destined to be who we are. Our mother was a hoe and our daddy was her trick, and they were both strung out. I smoke hella weed and will smoke a grimmy from time to time, but that ain't like that shit they was on."

They pulled up in front of an apartment building on 82nd and Birch Street. They got out of the car and Yesina said what's up

to the dudes that were standing outside. When they went in, the music was loud and weed smoke was thick.

"Hey, girl!" a lady yelled loudly.

"Hey, ma. This my sister, Lexi."

"Ain't she a cute lil' thang? You smoke?" She handed Lexi the blunt without questioning age or anything. Lexi hit it and passed it to Yesina. "Come on in, what you drinking?"

"Whatever you got," Lexi responded. She needed something to dull the pain of losing Bank Roll. "Wait, Sin, roll me somewhere real quick."

"Get ya cup and let's bounce." Sue made them both gin and juice, and they jumped in the car once more. "Where we headed?"

"I need to roll by Bank Roll's."

"Aight." They rode in silence and when Yesina pulled up in front of his house, she turned off the engine and told Lexi she'd wait for her outside.

She walked in the house and looked around. She knew it was a matter of time before it was all going to be gone, so she figured she would get her shit and leave. She went to the safe to empty it, but couldn't remember the combination to save her life. Her mind was scrambled and as she toyed around with different number combinations, nothing worked. She walked to the extra room that used to be hers and retrieved the twenty thousand dollars she had hidden in a loose floorboard next to the bed. After getting her money, she saw a folded piece of white paper. She picked it up and read it.

I knew you was smart, baby girl. No matter how good you think a nigga taking care of you, always keep a personal stash for a rainy day. Since I've discovered this stash, move ya shit to another spot.

She let out a small chuckle. She hadn't checked her stash in a while, so she had no idea when Bank Roll wrote the note.

"Why did you have to leave me?" she questioned.

She knew she would survive, but she had never anticipated Bank Roll leaving her so early. She thought back to the last time she saw him. He told her he had to make a few runs and told her

not to wait up for him because he wouldn't be in until late. She blew him a kiss, and he walked away from the front door and sat next to her on the couch.

"No matter what happens, you stay on track."

"OK, daddy," was all she said. She wondered why he chose to say that to her at that time, but he always told her to stay on track so she let it go.

He kissed her. "I love you." Lexi's eyes were wide. She had waited and dreamed of those words falling from Bank Roll's lips, but when they did she was speechless. He kissed her again. "I know, baby girl." Right before he turned to walk out of the door, he winked at her.

When she stretched and opened her eyes the next morning, he wasn't in bed. There were many times he didn't make it home so she got up, showered, and straightened the house. Later that day, Bianca was the one that dropped by the house.

"Hey, girl. I'm glad you came over. I was getting bored." It was summer so there was no school to keep Lexi occupied while Bank Roll handled business. "Come on in." She stepped to the side to let Bianca in. She began walking to the living room and noticed Bianca still hadn't said a word. Lexi's heart began to pound hard. She felt something was wrong. She turned around and for the first time and noticed Bianca's tear stained face. "B, what's going on?"

"There were some folks after him, but he didn't want you to know and get worried. They finally got him, Lex."

Lexi took a deep breath. "What do you mean?"

Bianca reached her arms out to hug Lexi. "I'm sorry, girl, he's gone."

It was a good thing Bianca's arms were already out because Lexi collapsed soon as her brain registered what she had been told. When she came to, she had to confirm what her heart already knew. "He's gone?" she questioned.

"I'm sorry, Lex."

She wanted to cry, but she couldn't. All she could do was replay his last words and look at that same door she last saw him at. It was almost as if he knew his time was up. She kept hearing him tell her he loved her, and she wished she had said more to him.

The next few days were a cluttered whirlwind as she did what she was supposed to do. She got his funeral together and let everyone know what was up. While everybody said their final goodbyes and thought they would sit and whisper while she sat right there, she said goodbye in her own way while leaving everybody with their mouths dropped open because she looked flawless. She laughed.

"I'm gonna do you proud, daddy."

Lexi packed shoes, clothes, and took everything that was important to her. Bank Roll's sister let it be known she was taking over his assets and Lexi didn't have time to argue with her old ass. She knew it was going to be a battle because Bertha had already given Lexi a stank attitude when she had been contacted. She didn't know how anyone could look down on her when their whole family had been hustlers, but nevertheless, she did her duties as his special bitch and left it at that. She took the picture from the wall that they took a few months earlier in Hawaii. She kissed her finger and put it up to his lips. "I love you, too, daddy" she whispered before she looked over the house once more and headed out of the door.

"Damn, did you get everything in that muthafucka?" Yesina asked as she helped Lexi put two heavy suitcases in the car.

"This ain't even half my shit, but I got the important stuff."

"Stay at the house with me tonight."

Lexi shrugged her shoulders. "That's cool. Sue not gonna mind?"

Yesina laughed. "Yea, right. She don't care about nothing that go on."

"I can't believe you been in the east and ain't even came to see about me," Lexi finally said. She never said it, but she missed her sister.

"I be in shit. I ask about you and shit. I knew you was doing hella good and I wanted you to keep doing good. This street life ain't shit." They headed back to 82nd Street, parked, and went in the apartment. There was a full house when they arrived. "Hey, babe." Yesina walked toward the guy and kissed his cheek. "This my sister, Lexi."

31

Todd grabbed Lexi and pulled her close, too close, for a hug. "Nice to finally meet you, lil' sis."

Lexi had seen that look in his eyes many times, and she was disgusted that she could tell he had thoughts of fucking her right in front of her sister and she said nothing. "Hey," Lexi said dryly.

Todd looked at her and smiled again. "You so damn sexy."

Lexi rolled her eyes. "Sin, let's walk outside." She pulled her sister's arm and led her outside. "So, really, that's your dude? That's why y'all stay fighting 'cause that nigga can't keep his dick in his pants, huh?"

"You just never been in love before. Bitches be throwing it at him, and I gotta check that ass. A nigga gonna always fuck if pussy right there. You gotta overlook that shit and know what you do to a nigga, can't no other bitch do."

Lexi shook her heard. "Whatever floats your boat."

As they stood outside talking and laughing, a light skinned girl walked up. "Where Todd?"

"Bitch, you got me fucked up," Yesina said before running up on the girl and started swinging. Before she could react, Lexi's instincts made her run up as well and help her sister stomp the girl out. Todd ended up running outside after one of the corner boys told him what was going on.

"Kim, why you always starting trouble?" he yelled as he pried the sisters off of the girl.

With a bloody nose, swelling eye, and busted lip, Kim screamed, "I wasn't starting trouble when we was just fucking!"

That did it. Yesina tore away from Todd and started pounding the girl again. Like déjà vu, Lexi jumped in once again. The rest of the corner boys helped pull the girls apart.

"Yesina ain't no damn joke," one of the boys said while laughing.

"She ride or die. You got a sister?" another yelled.

While Todd threw Kim in the car to take her home, he pointed at Lexi. "That's her sister right there."

The dude that asked the question approached Lexi. "Damn, lil' chocolate, what's up with you?"

32

"Not a damn thang," Lexi said, walking in the house with Yesina. "Who was that bitch?"

"His baby momma."

Sue shook her head. "Y'all gonna keep on fighting over that nigga, huh?"

Yesina smacked her lips and rolled her eyes. "That's my man, and that bitch can't have him."

"That's right, girl. Don't let nobody take your man," Sue egged with a Newport dangling from her lips.

Sue was thirty two and thought Todd was more her friend than her son. She let him raise himself and had no problem with letting little girls spend the night. That was how Kim got pregnant a year earlier because she kept telling her mother she was staying at her friend's house when she was laid up with Todd. Kim's mother was furious to learn her thirteen year old daughter was having a baby. She wanted her to get an abortion but she refused, and Planned Parenthood wouldn't make her if she didn't want to go through with the procedure. She was in love and wanted to have Todd's baby.

Kim was crushed when Yesina entered the picture. Todd forgot all about her and Toddeshia. Kim and Yesina fought every time they bumped into each other, which was often. Although Todd made it clear he wasn't Kim's man anymore, he stated he was her baby's daddy and he could hit it whenever he wanted. Kim let him fuck her whenever he wanted because she thought that was the way to get him back. She told herself she needed to move on, but Todd was her first and she loved him. As each day passed, moving to New Jersey with her aunt sounded better by the minute.

Once the dust settled, Lexi and Yesina hung out for a while and the hours crept by. It was three in the morning when Lexi was sleep on the couch and Todd finally walked in. He stood over Lexi, lusting after her young body. He sat down and slowly rubbed her leg. Lexi's eyes were closed, but she wasn't sleep. She was again disgusted. She pretended to stretch and turn over, and in the midst of doing that she kicked the shit out of Todd. He sat motionless and waited for her to settle again. He then slowly moved his hand under her cover to rub her leg. Lexi couldn't play the game.

She shot straight up. "Look, I would never fuck over my sister for a grimey ass nigga like you. You probably been fucking that bitch, then you wanna come over here and think you gonna creep in my panties, dirty ass nigga."

"You a feisty lil' thang, huh? Yea, your sister was, too, but I broke that ass down."

"You a bitch ass nigga and she'll see the light soon enough."

"Naw, that's my bitch and she will be forever."

Todd thought of taking the pussy but he knew Lexi would scream and fight, and that wasn't a good look. He vowed to catch her another time. He walked in the room and a few moments later, Lexi heard moaning from them fucking. She shook her head. She knew a woman in love could see nothing past her man. Before things got out of control, she grabbed her heavy ass suitcases out of the car and called a cab to take her to her to a motel until the next morning.

She hadn't been to Elizabeth's house in years. She was about nine the last time her and Yesina jumped on the bus and showed up. Derrick and Candy had been gone a full week and there wasn't any food left in the house. Yesina got up early that morning and washed them some shorts, a shirt, and clean panties, and hung the items over the fence in the backyard to dry. She washed and conditioned her and her sister's hair, and combed neat ponytails for both of them. She got a few dollars from Bank Roll and they jumped on the bus.

Yesina always wanted to make sure they looked their best when they showed up on Elizabeth's doorstep because everything there always looked good. The house was clean. There was always food. Elizabeth didn't even drink, let alone get high on crack.

Lexi shook her head. Yesina always took care of her. She marched right up to Elizabeth's house and knocked on the door. Chrisette opened the door, looked them up and down, and let them in. She had always been a bitch.

Christy walked up to the sisters. "Hey, Sin. Hey, Lexi. You guys spending the night?" she asked.

Chrisette rolled her eyes. "What you think? Uncle Derrick and that damn Candy probably out somewhere trying to get high."

Yesina looked at her and rolled her eyes. "Anyways, *Christy*, yea, we staying here long as Auntie OK with it." Both girls had that Savage fire in them. Chrisette talked shit to almost everyone in the family, but Yesina wouldn't take it and as Lexi got closer to the house, she knew she wouldn't take it, either. Chrisette had moved out but her and Christina visited their mother often, and Lexi was prepared to clown anyone that seemed to need it.

CHAPTER 5

Lexi walked up to that door as tall and as strong as her sister had done so many times. She knocked and waited to see who would answer.

"Hey, Lexi. What's up?" Christy said when she opened the door.

"Same shit, different day," Lexi said as she walked in the house like she owned it. "Where's Auntie Liz?"

"She at work. Where Yesina?"

"She ain't here." Lexi placed her suitcases on the floor and dropped her purse on the couch before she sat down. "You think it'll be cool to stay here a little while?"

"We got two empty rooms now. I'm sure momma won't trip. I need some company."

Lexi rolled her eyes and looked annoyed by Christy. "Y'all got anything to drink in here?"

"Some orange juice and Kool Aid."

Lexi laughed. "Bitch, I mean like vodka, gin, erk and jerk."

"You know my momma don't drink."

"Shit, you seventeen, don't you?"

"I...umm, yea...well, I had...I can..."

"You such a square. I hope you ready for me to turn your world out." Lexi walked out the door, went to the store on the corner, and got someone outside to buy her a fifth of gin. "What time Auntie get home?" she asked as she cracked open the bottle and made a drink.

"'Bout midnight."

"Good."

Lexi looked at the clock and saw it was only a little past four. She made Christy a drink and they got fucked up. By the time Elizabeth arrived home, they both were passed out on the couch. She saw the empty gin bottle and shook her head. She wondered what had happened that brought Lexi to the house. She sighed once more as she looked at her daughter and her niece. She knew it was going to be a long journey.

"My head hurt," Christy said when she finally woke up the next morning.

Lexi laughed. "Square ass bitch. Where my shit at? You been fucking with my shit?" she asked as she stood up and looked at Christy like she was ready to fight.

"No, girl." She looked at the clock. "Momma must have come home and took it upstairs."

Lexi narrowed her eyes. "For your sake, you better hope she had."

She went toward the back and looked in Chrisette's old room. Everything looked the same. She went to Christina's room, and saw her luggage on the floor and purse on the bed. Lexi let out a small laugh. Chrisette's bitch ass would never want anyone in her room. She entered the room and closed the door. She then checked her purse and suitcases to make sure nothing was missing. She knew Elizabeth wouldn't touch her stuff, but instincts made her check just because.

She pulled out a t-shirt, shorts, and got ready to shower. She knew things were about to change, and she had to prepare herself. She took a long, hot shower and as she walked back to the room she assumed was hers, she heard Elizabeth talking to Christy.

"I'm disappointed in you. Christy, you know better."

"But, momma, she was feeling down. I just wanted to chill with her and help her a little."

"Downing a damn bottle of gin helps nobody, and you know that. What you should have done was be an ear, let her talk to you. Sometimes, a shoulder to cry on and a good ear is the best medicine."

"I know, momma, but..."

"I'm going to overlook it this time, but you're a strong young lady. You are a leader, not a follower."

"Sorry I disappointed you," Christy said with her head down.

Weak ass bitch. Leader, huh? We'll see," Lexi thought as she waited a few seconds, and then knocked lightly on Elizabeth's cracked door.

"Come in, Lexi."

"Hi, Auntie Liz. I apologize for imposing on you, but I had nowhere else to go," Lexi said, looking like a lost little girl. While she was in the bathroom she braided her weave into two ponytails, making her look like a dark skinned Pocahontas. She had removed her eyelashes and her makeup to give Elizabeth the image she needed to see.

"You know my door is always open, but I have rules." Elizabeth patted the empty space on the bed next to her.

Lexi sighed lightly as she took her place. She had always thought Elizabeth Savage was the true definition of a boss bitch. Her husband cheated on her and she raised his bastard child. On top of that, when he died she never fucked with anyone else. She held down the house and the girls, and Lexi admired her for that. She wondered why Chrisette and Christina wilded out so much. She didn't know much about them, but she knew both had kids when they were teenagers and were always terrorizing some girl over a nigga. Lexi could be sure of at least one thing, they damn sure weren't punks.

She looked at Christy, the one that could have been her sister. She was so weak and pathetic. Everybody treated her like the punk she was, even her younger nieces. She wasn't sure how long she would stay, but she knew she would have fun running Christy.

"How are you doing?" Elizabeth asked. She pulled Lexi closer for a hug.

Lexi shrugged her shoulders. She wasn't sure how much Elizabeth knew about her life and she didn't want to give her any more than she already had. Bank Roll always told her she'd learn more from listening than talking. "I'm fine."

"I haven't seen you since the funeral. How you been holding up? Where's Yesina?"

"Sin's been fine. I was staying with someone in the neighborhood to stay at the same school. That's not cool for me no more, so I was wondering if it would be OK to stay here?"

"Honey, you know you're always welcome. Yesina is, too, if she needs somewhere to go. Next time you see her, you make sure you tell her that."

Elizabeth remembered how Yesina looked when she saw her last. She looked so much older and had bruises. She could tell the guy that stayed glued to her side was her pimp. Elizabeth wanted to snatch her up then, but she told her if she ever needed anyone or needed a place to stay that she always knew where to find her. She was glad Lexi felt comfortable enough to come to her before she got too caught up trying to be in the same wild streets that claimed her parents.

"That's means a lot, Auntie Liz."

"So, where are you in school?"

"I'm doing great. I'm ready to go to the tenth grade when school starts."

"Well, that's a good start. I'll start looking into getting you transferred. You and Christy can go to school together and she can look after you. Meanwhile, while summer is still here, there are some house rules."

Lexi looked up at Elizabeth like she was soaking up every word. "Yes, ma'am," she replied. Lexi knew how to flip the switch from grown woman to little girl in an instant.

Elizabeth gave her a warm smile. She thought Lexi was such an adorable little girl. She had heard about her living with the older man that was her pimp. When she looked in her eyes, she didn't see a wild girl who had been turning tricks and doing more than she had to at her young age. She didn't see a girl that had parents that cared more about their high than their kids. She saw a young girl that could be turned into an extraordinary woman if guided correctly, and that was what she planned to do. She knew it wasn't her fault, but she had always felt guilty that Derrick was in so much despair that he had turned to a young prostitute for empty emotions.

"We have chores around here. I work the swing shift at the hospital and I have to be sure I can trust you guys. I usually prepare dinner, but it's your job to keep your room clean, the kitchen, and living room. It's summer, so you're allowed to be out until ten and since I don't get off until eleven thirty, I'm trusting you girls will be in when you are supposed to."

"Yes, ma'am, I certainly understand. I really appreciate you giving me so much trust and I promise not to take advantage of it." Lexi gave her aunt that puppy dog look as she had done so many times to Bank Roll, and knew she had Elizabeth right where she wanted her.

"One more thing. I don't tolerate alcohol, cigarettes, or any illegal drugs in my home. We go to church on Sundays in this house, too."

"I understand, ma'am." Lexi reached over, gave her aunt a hug, and got up to leave the room.

"Christy, you know what I will and will not tolerate so I expect you to show Lexi the ropes."

"OK, momma." Christy hugged her mother and left the room as well. She closed her mother's door and looked at Lexi. "We have to be more careful from now on. Momma let us get off easy this time," she whispered.

Lexi rolled her eyes. "You're a rookie. I got this."

Christy felt offended. She had always been the good girl because she didn't want Elizabeth to get tired of her and give her away like her mother did. She knew her sisters had done a lot of bad shit, but she also knew her mother had to deal with them because they were her children. She was tired of being good. She was ready to show Lexi just how down she could be.

CHAPTER 6

It was a week after Lexi had moved in. Her and Christy walked to the store on MacAuthor Blvd.

"Damn, you a fine lil' chocolate thang. Why I ain't seen you around here before?" Meech asked. He was the leader of the pack of boys that stood in front of the store and you could tell. He was a caramel complexion, about five feet ten, and had jewels and gold that let Lexi know he was the boss.

Lexi rolled her eyes. It seemed her skin color automatically gave everyone the right to call her chocolate or something or the sorts. "I just moved here with my aunt and cousin," Lexi said in a sassy tone.

"You need to let me be your man. I can show you the world."

Lexi decided to switch her game plan and play with him. "You can?" Lexi asked with the same innocent eyes she had used on Bank Roll years ago.

"How old are you, lil' sexy?"

"Fourteen," she said shyly.

"You need to get on my team." Meech looked her up and down. She looked exotic to him.

Lexi shrugged her shoulders as she smiled. "I'll think about it, cutie."

While Lexi played her coy game with Meech, Christy talked to Buck, a guy she had been fucking for a few months. He looked dirty. He was five feet five and was stocky. His braids looked like they were past the point of needing to be done, and his

clothes didn't look as fresh as the other corner boys. That didn't matter to Christy, though. She wanted someone to love her and every time a boy showed any kind of interest, she gave him pussy. She was short and stubby. Although she had new clothes and kept her hair and nails done, all she ever seemed good enough for was a late night creep. No one wanted to make Christy their main girl, and take her out on dates and buy her gifts.

"How long your cousin gonna be around? She gonna be cock blocking?" Buck asked as she freely roamed Christy's body on the busy street.

Christy giggled. The only time she felt sexy was when a boy talked to her. Any boy. "She not blocking nothing. She cool."

"Call me later. We need to make a run." He tried to look important as he looked toward Meech. "Meech, we got that thang to do."

Meech looked at Buck and nodded his head. "Look, baby girl, I gotta make some moves."

Lexi froze for a moment. Baby girl was what Bank Roll always called her. She took a deep breath, put on her game face, and quickly gained her composure. "That's cool, daddy. I understand when a man has to make moves."

"What's your cell number?"

"I don't have one. Just call my cousin or something. You gonna call, right?"

Meech's head was gassed up from Lexi. "Imma come through tomorrow with something for you."

"I'll be waiting." Meech and Buck jumped in the gold Mercedes and rolled out. "Please, tell me you not fucking that dirty looking nigga," Lexi said as they walked in the store.

"He not...Buck cool."

Lexi frowned. "Ugh, so you *are* fucking him? I hella hope I just caught him on a bad day. How much money he give you?"

Christy laughed. "Ahh...Lexi, bitch, I been...these niggas know..."

Lexi raised her hand. "Just save that shit. You ready to roll with the big dogs or what?" Christy looked at Lexi and was ready to start her lying stuttering, but Lexi stopped her. "I'm about to show you some shit."

When Elizabeth got home, the girls were in the family room watching a movie and eating popcorn in their PJs. She knew Christy would be a good influence on Lexi.

The next night, Buck and Christy chilled in the car while Meech and Lexi sat on the porch. In his eyes, she was young and dumb. He vowed to fill her with so much cum she wouldn't know what to do. The day before when he asked for Lexi's cell number and she said she didn't have one, he knew the perfect gift for her. He proudly and presented her with a cell phone of her own and one hundred dollars to get her hair and nails done.

"Wow, thank you so much," Lexi said with enthusiasm. She acted like he had given her a gem that was precious and priceless.

Meech smiled cockily. "I told you I would show you the world being my girl. There is more of that if you act right."

"Oh, a phone? You shouldn't have. I've been wanting one of these things since forever." It was actually her first cell phone because she didn't feel the need for one. It was a nice trinket to have.

"There you go, lil' momma."

Lexi jumped on his lap and gave him a kiss. Meech had to pull back and get a hold of himself. He wasn't sure if Lexi was feeling him like that or what, but the kiss she gave him made his body tingle.

"Damn, lil' momma, how you learn to use that tongue like that?"

Lexi gave him a sly smile as she walked toward the house. She turned around and looked at Meech. "I know a few thangs about a few thangs." Meech jumped in the car as Christy got out and headed in the house. "What that nigga bring you?" Lexi asked.

"What you mean?"

Lexi smacked her lips. "Don't tell me you was over there suckin' that dirty ass nigga dick and you ain't even get shit from him."

"Who said...I wasn't...girl..."

Lexi gave her a straight face. "I know when a bitch sucking dick."

Christy let out a nervous laugh. "I was...just..."

"Look, I gives a damn how many dicks you suck. I'm just saying if you sucking dick, 'specially a dirty dick, you need to get paid. I ain't do shit for that nigga Meech and he gave me a phone, and a punk ass C note to get my hair and nails done." Lexi laughed. "Here, you can have this shit. At least you can say you at least got something from somebody." Lexi tossed the hundred dollar bill toward Christy and she quickly grabbed it.

"Damn, what you been doing to Meech?"

"Bitch, was you not listening? I just met the nigga yesterday, I ain't do shit." She turned to face Christy. "Yet. By the time I'm done, that nigga won't know what hit him."

They sat in the living room. "Lexi...umm, was you really..."

"What? Selling ass? At some point, we all sell ass whether we wanna admit it or not. For the most part, I wasn't a hoe on the streets or no shit like that. Bank Roll took care of me and he taught me how to be the coldest bitch out here. I got several ways to make money. Real money. If you got some sense, you'll watch and learn."

"I like fucking," Christy said out of nowhere. "I like the attention."

Lexi shook her head. "You need some self esteem. How long you been letting niggas fuck for free?"

"I been fucking about three or four years."

Lexi perked up. "So, who you been fucking?"

"I fucked a couple of my teachers. Dudes that be around my sisters' places."

"And, none of them niggas be paid?" Lexi asked as if she was in disbelief. She shook her head. "You just like my fuckin' sister. Out there chasin' nuts and shit. You betta get ya head on right."

"So what if I like fuckin'."

"You can lead a horse to water." Lexi went to her room. *Hmm, so that hoe been fucking teachers and shit, huh? She just need management. I need to see how strong my pimp hand is.*

Christy looked at the money Lexi gave her. *That bitch know she sucked his dick or something. He ain't just give her no*

money for a fuckin' kiss. I can get paid hella more than her young ass.

"Buck, lemme holla at you," Lexi said a couple of days later when she saw him at the corner store.

"What up."

Lexi crossed her arms. "How much is the pussy worth to you?"

Buck laughed. "I ain't paying for no pussy."

Lexi looked him up and down. He had trick written all over him. "Unless you tighten up your game, the only way you gonna get some good pussy is to pay for it. Now, unless you want me to clown you next time you around and make my cousin never talk to you, you better break me off two hundred."

Buck waved her off. "Bitch, you trippin'."

She got closer to him. "Try me. Not only will you not be lying up on my cousin's fat ass titties, no bitch around here will fuck you. You gotta pay to play, daddy," she said in a whisper.

Lexi walked in the store without giving him a chance to respond. When she left, she knew he was sitting in his car thinking hard. She laughed on the inside. He wanted pussy, so he was going to pay.

"You trying to fuck Buck tonight?" Lexi asked point blank when she got in the house.

"Yea, I need some dick."

"He gave you shit lately?"

"I told you I ain't tripping on none of that."

"We gonna play a little game with these niggas tonight. Straight up, you can't give a nigga all your time. There could be bigger, better niggas out there. We 'bout to go to the mall."

Christy looked like she was about to cry. "But, Buck said they was gonna come over around four or five."

Lexi gave her a look with her arms crossed over her chest. "Do it look like I give a fuck?"

"What if Meech give you some more money or something?"

"Read my lips. Do. It. Look. Like. I. Give. A. Fuck. Bitch, get dressed so we can bounce."

"I am dressed."

Lexi looked at Christy's attire. She had on jeans and a plain t-shirt with shiny black shoes. "Mary Poppins, you ain't going no damn where with me lookin' like that."

They went in Christy's room to find something. Nothing she had looked good to Lexi, so they went in Chrisette's old room to see if there was something there.

"Chrisette don't like nobody fucking with her stuff."

Lexi rolled her eyes and smacked her lips. "Chrisette bitch ass ain't here, is she? You need stand up for yourself. The bitch left her shit, so she must don't want it."

Going in her closet, Lexi found some things to work with. She found a cute shirt with shoes and a purse to match. She picked out a pair of dark Guess jeans Christy had.

When she came down the stairs, Lexi looked her over. She had braided Christy's hair the day before out of boredom and the blond mixed in looked good. Standing there with a gold and blue shirt that hung off one shoulder and gold sandals, she looked satisfactory. They could see anyone while they were out and Lexi wasn't going to be with anyone looking stupid.

"Damn, what you got on?"

Lexi had on booty shorts with a cut off shirt and heels. "Bitch, this is how you work it." The look had come straight from the latest video Lexi had seen and the girl was working it.

"We walking down MacAuthor with you looking like that?"

"What better way to come up? Let's go."

Lexi loved walking because she could check out the scenery, and see who was doing what and where. "Shit, I gotta find a nigga with a car," Lexi said. She knew she should have taken one of the cars Bank Roll had. She was owed that, but she let it be.

"Meech got a car."

Lexi gave Christy an annoyed look. "I'm sure I'll see people I know. Just be quiet and smile." When they got to the mall, they barely stepped in before Lexi saw Bianca.

"Hey, lil' momma. How you been doing?" Bianca gave Lexi a hug.

"What's up? I'm at my auntie house right now."

"You looking good." She smiled. "Devin been asking around for you."

Lexi raised her eyebrow. "Oh really?"

"It's been a few niggas wondering where you been, but he been wondering the most, girl." Bianca smiled.

"Good to know. What you doing after this?"

"Shit, I just ran up here to get my stamps. I'm 'bout to go burn one. Wanna roll?"

"Hell yea."

They went to the beauty supply, got a few things, and jumped in Bianca's Nissan Maxima. "Light this." Lexi lit the blunt and after she hit it, she passed it to Christy.

"I don't...umm..."

"Bitch, hit it."

Christy took the blunt and inhaled lightly. She coughed hard. "You a newbie?" Bianca asked.

"No...I...who said..."

"That bitch a square, giving away pussy and shit."

Bianca pulled up on the block and bought a few sacks of weed. They went to her apartment off Seminary Street and went inside. Christy looked around as if she was scared.

"Better hold your purse tight. It's gangstas around here." Christy's eyes got wide and she pulled her purse closer. Lexi laughed. "I swear." They went in Bianca's apartment and Lexi sat on the worn out couch while Christy stood. "Sit the fuck down, bitch." Christy looked at the couch where Lexi sat to the chair that didn't match. Feeling unity was better, she sat with her cousin.

Bianca came back from her room with a pack of cigarillos. "You the best roller. Hook it up," she said as she tossed the pack to Lexi. "Lexi, I don't think I ever told you how much I appreciate..."

Lexi waved her off. "Bank Roll would have wanted it. You held him down a long time. We fam."

When Bank Roll died, Lexi gave Bianca half of her money to help her out. She had kids and she needed the money more than Lexi. She also gave her the coke and ecstasy she found to sell or whatever. Lexi knew Bianca got down with ecstasy, so figured she would keep most of those for herself. Bianca had gone down to the

welfare office to get stamps and a check to hold her over until she figured out what she was going to do with her life. Plus, she still had regulars that knew they had to pay to play.

Christy's eyes got wide. "You be...umm..."

"Do she sell ass? Most def. She a bad bitch, too."

Bianca smiled proudly. "I was taught by the best."

Christy was blown away. She had never been around a real prostitute. Candy had been by their house every so often to wild out and pick up her kids, but she had never chilled with her. "You be out there fucking hella niggas?" Christy asked, trying to sound as hood as she could. She felt liberated to cuss in front of someone older than her and not get in trouble.

"As many as I need to in order to pay these bills and get high. Bank Roll never had me with random niggas, anyways. I mostly fucked balla niggas and a lot of them still come to see me."

"You ever fuck anyone you ain't want to?"

"Goes with the game. Long as you can make them niggas feel like they the best nigga you ever had and make they toes curl, the other shit irrelevant."

"You ever fuck a nigga that ain't wash his ass?"

Bianca blew out a breath. "Before I started fucking with Bank Roll, this one nigga name Toad stayed in my neighborhood and always wanted to fuck. He was always funky, too, but he paid so damn good. I just held my breath for as long as I could and made him nut as fast as I could."

"You ever fall in love with any of them niggas?"

"Damn, bitch, is you tryin' to audition to hoe or something? What's up with all the fuckin' questions?" Lexi asked as she finished rolling the last blunt and lit it.

"I was just curious."

Lexi looked at her cousin. She could see in her eyes that she wanted to walk on the wide side. "You got an itch, cuzzo? You want one of these hood niggas to scratch it for you?" She looked at Bianca and winked her eye.

"I...umm...I was just asking."

"Naw, you want some real dick, huh? Some thug dick. Bianca, call up Boo and tell him to come through."

"I don't...what you..."

"Girl, hit this damn blunt. Boo gonna hook you up right."

"What you want it to run for?" Bianca asked as Christy hit the blunt.

"The regular."

Boo was one of the dudes from the block that loved to buy ass. He had a big dick and was fine, but he wanted to spend money. He had once told Bianca he liked it better that way because he didn't have time to be tied down to a bitch asking questions and in his business. He was a freaky nigga and most times, by the time he got done the girl felt like they should be paying him.

The phone rang ten minutes after Bianca left the message. She told Boo she had some new ass at the house and asked was he down. "New ass? I'm on that."

When she hung up the phone, she looked at Christy and smiled. "Go jump in my shower, Boo like his bitches clean. Y'all can use my room."

"What you mean?" Christy asked, scared.

"Bitch, you just said earlier you wanna fuck. I got you. Go wash ya ass and Boo gonna come break you off," Lexi said like they were talking about a sandwich or something.

Christy was nervous and excited at the same time, but she shook off the nerves. It was time to let Lexi see she was ready to be down. The thought of taking a shower and waiting for some stranger that liked to fucked hoes made her tingle. She hit the blunt one last time and went to Bianca's bathroom.

"There are towels in the closet," Bianca yelled behind her. "Oh yea, I got some douches under the sink."

"Thanks," Christy replied. She looked under the sink. *Douche? What the fuck am I supposed to do with this?* She had never used one, but after looking over the box she figured it was to clean her pussy. She was clean, but figured she'd use one since Bianca suggested it.

"What's really going on?"

"Can't you see that shit all over her face? Her square ass wanna be down and she love getting some dick. You should see this busted ass nigga by her house. She been sucking and fucking that nigga for free." Bianca shook her head. "Shit, the bitch wanna give it up, we gonna get paid."

51

"Bitch, you ain't shit."

"Fair exchange is no robbery, you know that."

"You know Boo gonna turn her ass out."

"Yea, I know. And, he gonna make her wanna scratch that itch all the time. I got a lil' money, but I know Imma be bored out there at they house. Gotta have a little fun while I continue this education."

There was a knock at the door. Knowing it was Boo, Bianca said, "Come in, nigga."

Boo walked in and smiled. "Ahh shit, you gonna let me hit that shit, Lex?"

Lexi stood up and grabbed Boo's dick that was already hard. "Damn, you packed just like they say. Where you get all this dick from, daddy?" she whispered.

Boo smiled wide. "A nigga was just blessed. Damn, I been wanting to spread them thighs. What's up?" He licked his lips while he looked at Lexi's cleavage bursting from her top.

"Nigga, my cousin 'bout to serve you up. Matter of fact, give her that super freaky shit I heard you do. Act like you fuckin' me," Lexi said, and then licked his neck.

"You gonna throw that sweet ass pussy at me one day and I ain't even gonna fuck with you."

Lexi smacked her lips. "Yea, right."

"Nigga, don't be nutting all over my sheets and make sure you pick ya damn rubbers up when you done."

"You gonna let me tap that later tonight?" he asked Bianca.

"If you paying right."

Boo went in his pocket and gave Lexi two hundred dollars, and then went to Bianca's room. Lexi gave Bianca a hundred.

"That was the easiest money to date. Thanks, girl."

"Don't mention it."

Christy got out of the shower and although she tried to act like it was something she did every day, her nerves were in her stomach. She covered the front end of her body with the towel since it wouldn't fully wrap around her. She cracked the door and heard Lexi and Bianca laughing in the living room. She heard a male voice and assumed it was the dude they called Boo. She

eased the door closed again and took a few deep breaths. She was about to fuck some strange dude, and her pussy thumped and was wet from the thought of that. She took one more deep breath and went to Bianca's room.

Being it was summer at seven it was still light, but Bianca had a black blanket over her window, making it seem later than it was. Christy slowly walked in the room and saw Boo butt naked on the bed smoking a blunt. Her eyes almost popped out of her head when she saw his big ass dick. And, he was so fine. He was about five feet eleven with a butterscotch complexion. He had tight, Chinese eyes and had his hair braided. His six pack was banging and Christy wondered why he paid for pussy.

"Bring your thick ass over here," Boo said. Christy walked toward him and took the blunt from him like she was a pro. She needed to calm her nerves, so she inhaled deeply and gave it back. Boo freely roamed her body. "Damn, put one of them big ass titties in my mouth." Christy stood in front of him and put a nipple in his mouth. He bit it lightly before he sucked it hard. "Spread them legs." She parted her legs and he began playing with her pussy. "Damn, this shit already wet. You a freak, huh?"

"Yea."

"I like clean pussy. Lay on this bed."

Christy laid down and Boo opened her legs. He bent down and began licking her clit. Christy wiggled and moaned. She usually sucked dick and fucked, no one had tasted her before. Boo looked up, put the blunt in the ashtray next to the bed, and put Christy's legs over his shoulders. He licked her as he fingered her pussy. She moaned and put the pillow over her face to muffle her screams. She felt so good she didn't know what to do. He took his finger out of her pussy and inserted it in her ass.

"Shit, eat that pussy. Damn, baby. Give me that shit," Christy said, hoping she sounded right.

"You like that shit, lil' freaky bitch?"

"Yea."

"You want me to make this pussy cum?"

Christy wished he would stop talking and keep licking. She grabbed the back of his head and buried his face in her middle. She felt her stomach clench with butterflies. Boo licked her slow as he

fingered her ass. When she finally came, he stuck another finger in her ass and left both fingers there until she stopped screaming and shaking. He grabbed her hair and pulled her up until her mouth was at his dick. She wanted to make him feel the same way she had. She sucked his dick like her life depended on it, bobbing up and down, leaving spit to lubricate it. She had also been in Chrisette's X rated movies and she had learned a few moves from fucking.

"Damn, suck this dick. Take all this dick in your mouth."

Christy did all she could to suck up as much as his dick as she could. He squeezed her titties as she slurped him up. He pumped and pumped, and then busted his nut all over her face.

"Lay back," he said as he grabbed a condom from the dresser and put it on. Boo opened her legs wide as he could and stuck his dick inside her. Her pussy was so wet that he slid in with ease. "Damn, this some wet pussy. You like getting this pussy fucked, don't you?"

"Ummhmm," Christy moaned.

He worked her out for over an hour. Lexi and Bianca were in the living room cracking up. "When you think that bitch gonna want a hit again?" Lexi asked.

"Shit, I'm a pro, but Boo will make a bitch fall in love and shit. She know he paid you?"

"Hell naw, her dumb ass don't know." After a few moments of silence, Lexi said, "You know, she was almost my sister."

Bianca frowned. "How?"

"My daddy was fucking with her momma but she was cheating with his brother, my aunt husband. Auntie Liz a bottom bitch for real because she took that girl in and raised her damn near since she left the womb from what I heard. That shit drove my daddy crazy, though, and I guess that's how he ended up fucking with my momma. I loved my momma to death, but sometimes I can't help but wonder what if."

"Yea, I know what you mean. Life is crazy like that."

Lexi paused to hear the headboard hitting the wall and Christy screaming. "Damn, he breaking that bitch back or what?"

"Knowing Boo, he probably is. I'm hoping that nigga do come back through later on 'cause I need some dick."

"Bitch, don't tell me you caught up on a nut."

"Come on now. Best believe there won't be no nut if the money ain't right."

"Speaking of money, here's twenty if you can take drop us off. We on 82nd and Outlook. I'm faded and don't wanna deal with no bus ride."

"I got you."

They smoked and talked, and finally Christy and Boo emerged from the room. "Imma hit you up later, Bianca," Boo said as he walked out of the door.

"Later."

Christy dropped on the couch. "He fucked me so good. Damn."

"Wore that pussy out, huh?"

"Get outta la la land, bitch. We 'bout to head back to the house."

"Bianca, umm, can you give me Boo number? Or, give him mine," Christy said.

Lexi rolled her eyes. "Bitch, don't be jocking no nigga. Come the fuck on."

Christy stood there as if she was actually waiting for the number. Seeing Lexi and Bianca get their purses and walk out the apartment, she had no choice but to follow. She was sure she would see Boo again. At least, she hoped she would.

CHAPTER 7

Lexi had no idea how hot Christy was. She tried to play the innocent, perfect daughter in front of Elizabeth, but when she wasn't home Christy was ready to fuck anyone. Buck ended up paying for her pussy. He paid Lexi each time he wanted to get some or Lexi would make sure her and Christy were ghost when him and Meech wanted to come around. When they were at Bianca's, there were plenty of guys that came through to fuck Christy. She had no objections to threesomes and gangbangs. Lexi enjoyed selling her cousin. She never understood how easy it was until she tried it for herself. She liked it even better that she didn't have to do the smooth talking bullshit to get her to sell ass. She got paid and Christy had no clue. She was just being a freak bitch.

To make Christy feel special, Lexi bought her a few pairs of shoes and outfits for school. The shit Elizabeth had purchased for them wasn't fly in Lexi's book. Everybody had known her to be a top notch bitch living with a top notch hustler, and she wasn't going to school being anything less. At Fremont she was known, but at Castlemont she was just another new girl. Still, Lexi walked in like she owned the school while Christy was meekly behind her.

"Bitch, walk the fuck up," Lexi said when she noticed Christy was too far behind her.

There was laughter from a group of girls. "Fat girl trying to be fly."

Christy suddenly felt too exposed. The jean skirt seemed too short and she felt like she had too much cleavage showing. Her

singles didn't feel as fly as one of the girl's, although Lexi had just braided it about a week prior.

Lexi stopped and turned around. "Bitch, who the fuck you calling fat?"

"Not you, burnt brownie." The girls laughed more.

"Since I'm a lady Imma give you a pass, but just know you've fucked up."

"Lex, let's just go," Christy said, clearly scared.

"You scared of these hoes?"

"You would be, too, if you knew what was best," Christy whispered. "They run the Castle."

Lexi looked the group up and down, gave a smirk, and turned to walk off. "If I ever see you punk to a bitch, I will beat your ass myself."

"Punk...I wasn't...bitch, them hoes..."

"Save it, Christy. I got Mr. Johnson. You had him?"

"Yea."

The smile on her face let Lexi know he was a teacher her hoe ass had fucked. She gave her signature smirk. "Cool."

Lexi walked in her English class and found a desk in the front row. *He not too bad looking*, Lexi thought. He looked to be in his mid forties and was very tall. He was dark skinned and had a low hair cut. As Mr. Johnson introduced himself and told the students what they should expect for the year, Lexi never broke eye contact. She had on a skirt and sat with her legs wide open, exposing her naked pussy. Mr. Johnson kept looking, clearing his throat and loosening the neck of his shirt. Lexi played with him, slightly rubbing her pussy for him to see. She made it through class and laughed all the way to math. Her next two teachers were old women, and then there was a teacher that looked to be close to death. Her history teacher was another teacher she wanted to play with. She did the same to him simply because there was nothing better to do. Mr. Forrest didn't find her antics too funny, although, he still looked. Finally unable to take her taunting, he sent her to the principal's office.

"What you sending me there for?" Lexi asked as the class eyeballed her.

"That skirt is too short, young lady."

Lexi rolled her eyes. "Yea, right."

She slowly walked to the office. When a student worker looked up, the same one that had taunted Christy earlier, she said, "I'm here to see the principal."

"I see we're starting off on a good foot already." She looked around to make sure no one was in earshot. "Look, little girl, I don't know where you came from, but I run this school. You and your fat ass cousin stay out of my way and we'll be good."

Lexi gave her another smirk as she looked her up and down. "I'll think about it."

"Mr. Mackey don't like sluts and you look like queen slut. Hopefully, he'll expel your ass." She was cute, but she wasn't shit in Lexi's book. She had on tight jeans and a white button up shirt with white sandals. Her burgundy weave was flat ironed to perfection and she had long, acrylic nails.

Lexi shrugged her shoulders as she walked in the office. "Take a seat, Ms. Savage," Mr. Mackey said without looking up from the computer screen. "I understand you transferred here from Fremont."

"Yes, sir," Lexi said, uninterested.

"Ms. Savage, there are certain things we don't tolerate here." He finally looked up for the first time. "We expect young ladies to dress appropriately."

"I've seen plenty of girls with skirts the same length or shorter than mine. What's the problem?" she said as if she wasn't speaking with an adult.

"Mr. Forrest has been here for a long time. I can't recall a time he has sent someone to the office for their attire."

"So, you want me to do what?"

"Looking at your records, your academics are highly impressive. I'm not sure what the problem is, but let's not make this a habit of you visiting my office."

"Got cha." As Lexi bent to pick up her back pack, that was when she saw the lust in Mr. Mackey's eyes. She made a mental note of that look.

"Thank you for being so easy on me, Mr. Mackey," Lexi said as she expertly batted her eyelashes and gave him the sweetest

smile he had ever seen. She slowly walked out of his office, knowing he watched as she put an extra sway in her hips.

After school, Lexi met Christy in front of the school to go home, and was surprised to have Meech and Buck waiting on them. Lexi laughed to herself. Meech had been on her hard. While Christy was fucking and sucking Buck every chance she got, Lexi kissed Meech every now and again and they fondled each other a little. He thought she was a little girl that was scared, so he tried not to pressure her for sex. Plus, he had plenty of girls he was fucking. Lexi was special, and he wanted her to give it to him when she was ready.

As slick as Lexi was, she made sure to let Buck know not to tell Meech, or anyone, that he was paying to get fucked. She made him feel as if it was a privilege and truth be told, Buck didn't want anyone to know he was paying for pussy, anyways. He often wondered if Meech had to pay, too. He figured if he wasn't giving her cash, the presents he gave Lexi was payment enough. In less than two months he had bought her outfits and shoes, given her chains and rings, and stuffed animals. He acted like a nigga in love instead of the player Buck thought he was.

When Christy walked to the car, Buck got hard when he saw her in the short skirt. She was nice and thick, just the way he liked them. Other dudes always clowned and said she was fat, but what Buck saw was thick legs, big titties, and a round ass.

"I didn't know you was coming to pick me up," Lexi said as she got in the car.

"I can't have my boo walking. I got you, ma."

"Hell, how 'bout a ride in the mornings?" They didn't live too far from school, but Lexi figured since the nigga was trying to act like he was doing big things then she was going to take it all the way there.

"You should have told me."

"Hey, baby," Christy said to Buck. She couldn't wait to get home and fuck.

Lexi shot Buck a look in the rearview mirror. She taxed him that first time, but since it was a game she told him after that he only had to pay twenty dollars. Lexi didn't know if Buck

thought she was dangerous or if he liked the thrill of paying for pussy, but he always had a twenty ready for her.

As they pulled from the curb, Lexi saw the girl from earlier that had tried to clown Christy and was the student helper in the office. "What's that bitch name?" Lexi asked Christy as she pointed, but Meech answered.

"That's Keedra, this chickenhead from around the way."

Lexi wasn't expecting him to answer, but that led her to ask another question. "You fucked her?"

Meech let out a laugh that let Lexi know he had fucked her. She looked at him because she knew he was about to lie. "Naw, she all on my dick, though." When Lexi didn't say anything, Meech continued. Again, she knew being quiet would benefit her more than asking another question. "I mean, I let her suck my dick once, but that's it. She think 'cause she a cheerleader everybody want her." Lexi looked out the window like he wasn't talking to her. "But, fuck her. I got something for you."

Lexi finally perked up. "You do?"

"Yea, Imma drop y'all at the house and come back."

"OK."

About five minutes later they pulled up in front of the house, and Lexi and Christy got out. "I'll be back in about ten."

"Cool."

The girls went inside. "How much you know about that Keedra chick?"

"Nothing 'cept she think she the shit. All the niggas in school at her. She's a straight bitch."

"Did you know she was trying to fuck with Meech?"

"I saw him pick her up from school a few times last year."

Lexi dropped on the couch. "This school shit is for the birds. It don't mean nothing to me no more since Bank Roll ain't here."

"I got Mrs. Watson for math. She the hardest teacher. Then, I got Mr..."

"Bitch, shut up." Lexi couldn't believe how annoying Christy could be. She was a total leech, trying to do anything she could to fit in.

Christy went to the kitchen and warmed up the lasagna her mother had made earlier. "You want some of this?"

"Naw, too heavy for my stomach. Maybe after I smoke this blunt." Lexi was about to go outside to smoke when she saw Meech pulling up. *I don't care what this nigga got, I'm about to fuck him and make him think he blew my mind. Bitch ass Keedra gonna try to clown somebody. I got something for her bitch ass.*

"Hey, daddy," Lexi said as she walked toward the car with a wide smile.

Meech reached in the back seat and gave her the bag. She opened it to see shoes and clothes. There was a smaller box that she took out and found diamond earrings. They were smaller than the ones Bank Roll had given her for her birthday, but Meech was a smaller nigga. Not impressed, she still threw her arms around his neck.

"You're so good to me."

"I'm feelin' you, lil' momma. I want you to be my girl."

Lexi gave a surprised look. "You do?"

"Yea. I'm always thinking about you, always want you around me."

"I feel the same way, daddy." She moved her hair to the side and kissed his cheek.

"Damn, I like the way you said that."

Lexi grabbed his hand. "You about to like something else." She led him to her room. "Sit right here," she instructed him.

Christy and Buck were already in her room fucking. Lexi slyly checked the jar on the end table in the living room and saw the bill in there, so everything was straight.

Meech sat on Lexi's bed listening to Christy moan and grunt. Her bed squeaked loud and fast. He hoped Lexi was finally ready to give him some pussy. He got the clothes and shoes from a booster, and the earrings he had bought for Keedra but she had been acting up so he gave them to Lexi.

He thought about Keedra. She was so fine, but her attitude was nasty. Almost as nasty as she was. She sucked his dick and let him fuck her however he wanted it, even in the ass, but she always had her hand out, always expected something. She was young in the mind and he was tired of her. Lexi was something different.

She was only fourteen, but she held herself like a woman. She actually had shit to talk about and no matter how hard he pushed up on her, she didn't slut herself out. She made him respect her, chase her.

When she went entered her room again, Meech had no idea what was in store. She had on a houserobe but as soon as she closed the door, she opened it and dropped it to the floor. She stood in front of him with a black bra and panty set. Meech licked his lips as he took her in.

"Damn, baby," he said.

"I been wanting you for a long time, but I had to be sure I was ready, that you were worth it," Lexi said softly.

"So, what you think?"

Lexi walked closer to him and kissed him. "Can I have you?" she asked.

"Shit, hell yea," he answered as he put his arms around her and began rubbing her smooth skin.

She laid him back and got on top of him, continuing the kiss in the process. She straddled him, grinding on him as they kissed more. Meech rubbed her smooth body, grabbing her ass and pulling her closer to him. She blew his mind like a seasoned pro. She pulled up his shirt and took it off, and then kissed his chest. She went down lower, and slowly unzipped his pants and helped him take them off. She took his dick out through the hole in his boxers, and then hesitated on actually sucking his dick.

"I'm not too good at this, so let me know if I'm doing it right," she said to him. She kissed him a little more, and then kissed and licked on his dick a little.

"You don't have to, baby." Meech tried to lift her up.

"No, daddy, you been so good to me, I want to thank you." She smiled at him again, driving him wild. He wasn't expecting much, so he planned to let her play around for a little while and then blow her back out.

She kissed and licked a little more, and then sucked lightly on his head. Meech had a nice sized dick, about eight inches, and it was pretty thick. Lexi knew she was going to have a good time. She played the shy and timid role for a little while longer. "Am I

doing it right?" she asked as she looked at him and licked him like a lollipop.

"Yea, you good, baby."

She sucked the head, and then sucked more of his shaft until she heard him moaning. She gathered some saliva in her mouth and used it for her lube. She sucked a little more, and then began to stroke his dick with her hands as she did so.

"Damn, baby, keep doing that shit." Meech's breathing was heavy and Lexi knew she had him right where she wanted him.

She sucked and stroked, taking a little bit more in her mouth each time. Meech grabbed the back of her head and pushed it down further. She sucked until his entire dick was in her mouth.

"Fuck, baby. Suck this dick. Suck all this shit. Damn. Fuck." Lexi knew when he yelled out anything that came to mind that it was a wrap.

Meech rambled random words, caught in her abyss. He could have sworn she was a virgin, but they way she sucked his dick he knew she had to have done it before. Lexi felt him swelling and knew he was about to cum, so she stopped.

She looked at him with innocent eyes. "Was that OK?" she asked as she batted her eyelashes as if she didn't know he was about to nut.

Meech didn't know if he was happy or pissed that she stopped. He knew he was about to bust a major nut in her mouth if she hadn't stopped, but he wanted to let go of his load in her pretty little mouth. "Goddamn, girl. What you trying to do to a nigga?" he said as he looked down at her innocent face.

"I just want you to like me," Lexi said sweetly.

"Shit, a nigga gonna love you if you keep that shit up."

"Can I suck it some more?"

"Take off them panties and bra." She did as told, and then Meech put her on the bed and put them in a 69 position. "I been hella waiting to taste this pussy." He stuck his tongue deep in her nectar as she grinded on his face.

"Mmm, daddy, I like that," she whispered.

She took him in her throat again, sucking him with no remorse. In return, he licked and sucked her clit like they were having a competition. Finally, she sucked his head as she jacked

his shaft, making him explode. She jacked his dick until he spurt out every drop. Ready to feel her own nut, Lexi sat up on his face and rode it until she came as well as she pinched her nipples.

Meech laid her down and was about to enter her. "Wait, you gotta put on a rubber."

"Come on, baby. I'm good."

Lexi shook her head. "No glove, no love."

"Shit!"

Meech got up and knocked on Christy's door. "What?" she said.

"Y'all got some rubbers in there?"

"Naw, nigga."

Lexi shook her head. Not only was her cousin a hoe, she was letting niggas run up in her raw. Lexi thought she was so stupid.

Meech returned to the room. "Baby, I promise I won't nut in you so you don't get pregnant."

Lexi was out of the bed and already putting her robe bac on. "Do I look stupid? Just 'cause you pull out don't mean you ain't got shit you can pass on to me."

"OK, Imma run to the store real quick."

Lexi shrugged her shoulders. She was ready to feel him, especially after seeing what he was packing, but she knew once he returned from the store it would be all bad. It would teach him to be better prepared in the future.

CHAPTER 8

It had been a week since Lexi was seconds away from giving Meech a mind blowing experience. He had been after her since then, ready for the pussy he felt was owed to him. She didn't appreciate him being unprepared, so the wait started over. Lexi wasn't pressed. She enjoyed sex and the way having an orgasm made her feel, but she could please herself. Bank Roll had taught her a nigga would never learn if she didn't teach them correctly. Class was in session.

Lexi and Christy were at Bianca's house. That had become their chill spot when Lexi wanted to get away from the goody goody house of Elizabeth Savage. She loved her aunt, but it wasn't the life for her. The life for her was in the mist of the hood with Bianca, and she taxed niggas that wanted freaky ass while she got high with her girl.

"Man, your cuzzo the freakiest bitch on the block and she ain't even on the block. Bank Roll would have made paper off her." Christy was in the back getting fucked by two dudes.

"I know, right? Who would have thunk Mary Poppins was fuckin' like that?"

"What's up with them sisters of hers?"

"Them bitches is crazy. Christina is aight, she used to keep us when we were little but I don't really remember, but that bitch Chrisette, she a fuckin' nut case. She told Christy she was a product of their dad cheating. I remember being there at the time when she said that shit. That bitch hella heartless."

"Shit, looks like it run through y'all veins. You ain't no can of peaches yourself," Bianca said, looking toward the back.

"Maybe that's why she always give me that look. She know we too much alike."

"Yea, y'all would butt heads too much."

"I'm so glad she shacked up with some nigga. She come over and give me the stare down. I stare right back and dismiss that messy bitch. She hella mean to Christy, though, and Christy always kissing her ass that much more. I'll say some slick shit on her dumb ass behalf, then Christy be all shitty with me 'cause Chrisette clown her harder."

"What you think your aunt gonna do if she ever find out what's going on?"

"She work second shift. By the time we home from school she leaving for work. On weekends, by the time we really up and about she leaving. Works perfect for me."

"You know, I'm real proud of you staying in school. You know I dropped out when I was in the tenth grade. You're smart, at least get your high school diploma. I'll be there at your graduation cheering the loudest when you do."

"I been looking into this GED thang. School OK, but I got bigger things on my mind and it's only gonna hold me back. I do want the papers, but I don't wanna do these years. I'm getting tired of being at my aunt house. Going to church and all that jazz is getting old."

"You know Bank Roll wanted you to graduate and go to college."

Lexi looked away from Bianca. "Yea, I know, but he ain't here no more. I feel like it's all for nothing."

"It's something. It'll be something for you."

"I feel you, but I got other shit on my mind right now."

"You know what, lil' sis, do what you gotta do." Bianca knew there was no changing Lexi's mind once it was made, but she hoped she at least tried to do the right thing for just a little while longer.

"Bank Roll gave me game I will have forever and it's coming close to me to use it."

Bianca looked at the time. "Girl, it's nine, you better get that cousin of yours and get home."

"I can smoke one more blunt if you take us home," Lexi said, knowing Bianca would accept.

Bianca smiled. She always had company, but she didn't have friends. Although Lexi was so much younger than her, she had been the one around for years and she hadn't done anything scandalous like fuck her baby daddy or start any bullshit. They spent hours talking, smoking, drinking, and just did things that girls did. They went to the nail shop together and went shopping. Plus, Bianca related to Lexi. She didn't have her father around, and mother was strung out and left her out to fend for herself at a young age. Having a baby to take care of made her have to fend for herself more. She wanted so much more for Lexi, and she knew Lexi had the tools to accelerate herself. She felt living with her aunt was a positive for her, and she wanted her to stay there long as possible.

"One more blunt, Lexi, then I gotta take you guys home." She looked toward the back. "Y'all wrap that shit up back there!" she yelled. "That bitch been fuckin' since we got here."

Lexi shook her head. "She'd keep on fucking until someone brought it to a stop. That shit is crazy how bad she like to have that itch scratched."

When Bianca pulled up in front of the house, Meech was waiting. "Where you been?"

Lexi frowned. "What?"

"I been back and forth over here all day."

"I been chillin'."

"I been tryin' to fuck with you."

Lexi rolled her eyes. "Psshh. You got many bitches on your jock. You ain't worried about me."

"I been doing everything I know to get close to you. I keep a pack of rubbers on hand and you been kickin' me to the curb. What's up? You fuckin' somebody else?"

"What if I was? You really think keeping a pack of fuckin' rubbers is the way to get close to me?" She let out a disgusted gust of air.

"You good, girl?" Bianca asked, not sure if she should drive off or not.

"Yea, go pick up them babies and get home, girl."

"Call me."

"I got you." Lexi turned to walk in the house.

Meech grabbed her arm. "Wait."

She snatched back. "Nigga, is you stupid? I'm not your girl. You may be able to grab on Keedra like that, but don't fuck with me." Her fists were balled and she was ready to fight. One phone call and Meech would be good as fucked up.

Meech exhaled. He was feeling Lexi and didn't want any problems. "I'll be here in the morning to pick you up for school." Lexi rolled her eyes and went in the house.

"I'm so tired. I need to hop in the shower and go to bed."

"Yea, you need a double shower, slut." Lexi rolled her eyes and went to her room. Meech had fucked off her high and her mood.

The next morning, Meech sat in front of the house waiting for Lexi. "New car, huh?" Lexi said as she got in the front seat and sat as close to the door as she could.

"Come on, Lex, don't be like that. You just got a nigga gone. I been trying to holla at you and show you I'm feelin' you, and you been playin' a nigga."

Lexi scooted a little closer. "I'm feelin' you, too, Meech. I know how you dope boys be having a flock of women. I don't want to be a notch on your belt. I don't want my heart broke."

Meech melted. In all his twenty two years, he had never heard something so sincere. When he pulled up to the school, he parked and turned off the car. "I got you, lil' momma."

"You coming to pick us up?" Lexi asked.

"Naw, Imma meet you at the house later."

Lexi smacked her lips and crossed her arms across her chest. "If I'm there."

Meech removed the key from the ignition and gave it to Lexi. "You'll be there, lil' momma. This is my gift to you."

"What?"

"Sometimes I'm busy. I can't always guarantee I can pick you up or drop you off, so I'm giving you your own way."

Lexi took the keys. *It'll do.* It was an older model Honda Accord with tinted windows and a CD player. "See you later." Buck pulled up in Meech's car a few moments later.

As Christy and Lexi walked toward the school, Christy said, "Did I just hear right? Meech gave you a car?"

"That would be correct, cousin," Lexi answered cockily.

"Damn, I thought you said you ain't fuck him yet?" Christy was jealous. She had done more than her share of fucking and sucking, and all she got was a nut. Most of the time it was a good nut, but no one gave her money or gifts, not even Buck.

Lexi smirked. "I haven't."

"Meech must be really feelin' you to give you a car and not fuck you yet." Christy felt like Lexi was lying, but she knew her cousin had no reason to lie.

"Bitch, you lying." Lexi whipped around to see Keedra standing behind her.

"Bitch, I don't think anybody was talking to you," Lexi said with a smirk. She knew Keedra had to be steaming.

"Meech ain't give you no damn car," Keedra challenged. She had been fucking him for a couple of years and although he gave her some nice gifts, none of them was anywhere near a car.

Lexi looked Keedra up and down. She was the typical cheerleader type. She, again, had on skin tight jeans with a hot pink tee shirt with a big sunflower on it. Her hair was done in Shirley Temple curls and her makeup was done to perfection. Her five feet six frame couldn't be more than one hundred and fifteen pounds of dark skinned beauty.

He likes the chocolate girls I see, Lexi thought. "Look, honey, I don't have time to play little girl games with you. If Meech was worried about you, he wouldn't be sniffing so hard up my pussy."

She looked at Lexi like she was disgusted. "He don't even like little girls."

"Which explains why he not fucking you anymore," Lexi shot back. Keedra got mad and slapped Lexi. "You got it, pom poms." Lexi turned and walked off without another word.

"Lexi, you gonna let that shit slide?" Christy asked.

"Bitch, hell no. Oh, she gonna get hers, believe that. Just not right now."

"What you mean?"

"Don't worry about it. You just go to class."

Lexi walked off like she didn't have a care in the world. She got to her first class and teased her teacher as she had every morning. It was getting harder for him to hide his erections and she wondered if her classmates saw what was going on. She had done a little homework and found out Keedra was his student helper during another period. She was about to change that. Lexi also knew the next period was Mr. Johnson's free period. She was glad she always listened and did homework. She found out so much about students and staff.

When the bell rang, Lexi took her time gathering her things. Once she was the last student in the class, she spoke. "Mr, Johnson, I need some help."

"What can I help you with Ms..." He stopped mid-sentence when he turned and saw Lexi with her legs fully opened, exposing her glistening pink middle.

"I think you should close the door," Lexi said lustfully.

Obeying, Mr. Johnson closed the door and locked it. He had daydreamed about Lexi since the first time she walked in his class. She always wore those short skirts or shorts with shirts that hugged her body. She always looked at him as he tried to teach the class with lust in her dark bedroom eyes. He wanted her so bad.

Mr. Johnson walked to Lexi's desk and stood in front of her. "What do you need help with, Ms. Savage?"

She looked at his erection. "Actually, I want to help you, daddy." In a swift motion, she undid his pants and had his dick in her mouth before anything else could be said. She deep throated him perfectly, making him erupt within minutes. Holding firm to the eye contact she always kept, she looked at him as she swallowed every drop of his cum. "There's more of that for you, but you have to do something for me."

Mr. Johnson was still shaking. Christy and other school girls had sucked his dick plenty of times, but nothing compared to what Lexi had just done. "Anything," he finally said.

"I don't want Keedra Tate doing IWE for you anymore."

"Why?"

"That doesn't matter. Get her off that and I have a special surprise for you." Lexi stood from her desk and kissed Mr. Johnson's cheek. "Mmm, I can't wait to taste you again, daddy" she whispered.

Mr. Johnson's skin tingled. He had been divorced for years and hadn't dated much. He sexually satisfied himself with students that were failing in class and ready to give him pussy, but they were never as sexy or experienced as Lexi. He could almost feel her insides. He could feel her hot juices coating his dick. If she wanted Keedra Tate gone, that's what would happen.

Being that the next period had already started, the halls were quiet. Lexi slipped out of the classroom and went to the bathroom to rinse out her mouth. On her way to her next class, she was told she needed a pass to get in since she was late. Not having one, she was sent to the office. She was glad it was too early to run into Keedra, she wasn't ready for her just yet.

After school, she sat out front waiting for Meech and then Christy reminded her about the car. "Damn, I forgot that fast."

"Do you know how to drive?"

"I know how to do everything."

"Momma gonna trip about you having a car, 'specially since you don't have a license and not even old enough to drive," Christy said on the ride home.

"I'll keep it parked around the corner."

"You fuckin' Meech now, right?" Christy hadn't known of Lexi to fuck one time since she had moved in, and she knew she wasn't the sweet little girl she pretended to be. She was ready to see the wild, hoodrat emerge.

Lexi rolled her eyes. "Girl, please. That's just what that nigga expect is for me to throw pussy at him. Not!"

"What if he take the car back?"

"He won't."

Lexi parked around the corner and they walked in the house. It was almost as if they lived by themselves since Elizabeth wasn't home when they were. Even on her off days, she managed to be out and about, visiting friends and or picking up extra hours. She trusted them so much.

An hour after being home, Meech arrived with someone new. "Hey, boo, this Slim. Slim, this my boo and her cousin, Christy."

"I remember you. I seen you around school a few times before I stopped going," Slim said to Christy.

She gushed at him recognizing her. "Hey, Slim. I remember seeing you a few times, too."

Everyone that saw Slim knew exactly why he had that name. He was tall and slim, nothing but skin and bones. He stood six feet one, and weighed one hundred and sixty pounds. Lexi saw the way Christy salivated and already knew she was ready to give him some pussy. Lexi shook her head.

"So, how was it being able to jump in your own ride?"

"It was cool, I guess," Lexi said, sounding uninterested. "Where Buck?"

"That nigga got knocked after he picked me up. He gonna be gone at least a year."

"Damn."

"Y'all thirsty or something?" Christy asked.

"I'm a lil' thirsty," Slim said.

Meech had already told him how she fucked and sucked Buck all the time, and they knew if Buck could get it Slim could. Plus, Meech needed someone to keep Christy out of his way. He couldn't try to get in Lexi's panties if Christy was all in their face. She played hard to get since he didn't have rubbers that first time, but he knew the car was an instant panty dropper and Buck being gone wasn't going to stop him. Christy walked in the kitchen and Slim walked behind her. Lexi made a mental note to get at him later.

"Let's go in your room," Meech said.

"What about your peeps?"

"Christy got it."

"She do, huh?"

Meech laughed. "You know she do."

She grabbed his hand and walked to her room. She laid Meech on her bed, got on top of him, and began kissing him as she grinded on his dick. Meech lifted her skirt and palmed her ass. Lexi took off her shirt and bra, and let Meech suck her nipples. She

74

wanted him, but he had to learn. He was ready to take off her panties.

"Oh, baby, I got my period."

Meech exhaled loudly. "Shit!"

"It's OK, baby, I'll take care of you."

Lexi kissed down his stomach and opened his pants to free his dick. She felt the box of condoms in his pocket and smiled. He should have thought of that weeks ago when she was ready to give him the best dose of pussy he ever had. She kissed and licked him slowly, just as she had the first time. She looked at him and smiled, getting more aggressive with her sucking. Meech grabbed her head, loving the way her mouth felt. She moaned while she sucked him, and that turned him on even more. She stroked his dick while she licked his balls. Meech was ready to explode, but he wanted to savor her just a little more since he knew he couldn't fuck. Going in for the kill, she gave him a good sucking until he exploded.

They lay in bed afterwards. "Hey, my birthday is next weekend. What I get?"

"Damn, ma, I just gave you a car."

"You didn't know my birthday was coming up, though, so that doesn't count."

"You a feisty lil' thang. That's what keep me interested in you, lil' momma. You don't take no shit and I like that."

"You used to bitches giving you the pussy, huh?"

They heard the moaning coming from Christy's room and knew she was in there fucking Slim. "Your cousin don't waste no time, do she?"

"You knew that, that's why you brought Slim over. You figured he'd keep her company while you tried to get some pussy, huh?"

Meech laughed. "I'm an open book. Buck also told me you was taxing him to hit that pussy. You gonna tax Slim?"

"Of course. I'm surprised Buck told you he had to pay to play."

"So, that's what going on here? You seeing how much Imma pay before I get to play?"

Lexi smirked. "What do you think? Anyways, Slim got a free shot this time, but if he not paying he don't get no more of her freaky ass."

"You a hustla, I like that, too. I ain't even mad. So many bitches give it up for free.

Meech wasn't lying. He liked the hustla in Lexi, but he wasn't about to be tricked out by a young girl. He was going to tear her pussy up, having her fiending for the dick, and then he was going to leave. Keedra was a gold digger, but she was up front with what she wanted. They usually all were up front with what they wanted. Meech thought Lexi was different. Almost.

Lexi could sense Meech was on to her. She decided to do something she never thought she would. She took a deep breath as if she was in thought on something serious. "I'm here at my aunt's house because my mother and father were killed by a dope boy they had robbed. They would leave me and my sister alone for days at a time, and my aunt would take us in whenever we came knocking at her door. We had done things you could never imagine to survive. All I know is hustling, and then I met you. I like you. I like you more than I've liked anyone, and that scares me." Her voice was so soft and the tone was so sincere that Meech had no choice but to bring her in for a hug as she allowed her eyes to become watery.

"I been through a lot of shit in life, too. I never knew my dad, but my momma has met so many losers in life, it's crazy. I've had more uncles than I can count. All them niggas did was come in and do nothing. She put me out when I had a fight with one of her dudes that was talking to her crazy. Imagine that. I bounced from house to house, hustling and shit till I got it together."

"We're two lost souls that were meant to be." Lexi didn't tell many people her business, but she always knew connecting with someone on some 'poor lost girl' shit was priceless. Almost everyone had a sob story, and if she told a roundabout version of hers at the right time, it got her where she needed to be.

He hugged her closer and kissed her forehead. "Maybe you're right, lil' momma."

"I don't want you to feel like I'm hustling you, but it's all I know. I promise to try to change that."

76

"It's cool. I know it's survival of the fittest in this game. You got all the tools, baby, and us together, we can be an untouchable team. Take a chance on me, I got you."

Lexi laid her head on his chest. "OK," was all she said. "Please, don't hurt me."

"Never that."

Lexi smiled. *Niggas are so simple*, she thought as she got ready for her next move.

CHAPTER 9

Keedra hated that Meech was with Lexi. She couldn't believe he wanted to fuck with that young girl over her. She had been calling him over and over, but he ignored her. Everyone knew that Meech had given Lexi the car she drove and that pissed Keedra off more as she heard the whispered gossip in the school halls. With Mr. Johnson telling her he didn't need her as his assistant anymore, she was forced to take on another class. She tried to fuck him to get him to change his mind, but he wasn't interested. She knew she would have to step her game up to keep things how she liked.

When Lexi found out Mr. Johnson did as she asked, she fucked him so good he almost cried. The power that pussy actually held amazed her. She wondered why there weren't more women pimping because it was absolutely true, pussy ruled the world. Bank Roll was a smooth nigga and he could sell salt to a snail, but still, women had what niggas needed in life. Niggas would do anything for hot, wet pussy and a pretty face. The problem was, most women didn't know that.

She had one more nigga in the school to conquer.

She had been in the principal's office a few times for petty stuff like talking back to her teacher or being late for class. Looking at her records, Mr. Mackey didn't understand what was going on. He wanted her to stay out of his office because she was so irresistible. Although it was against his job ethics, he had fucked a few girls in school but most of them were seniors. He figured it was a perk with his position that he fully enjoyed.

During lunch, Keedra and her gang walked by Lexi and Keedra bumped her, causing her to drop her things. Her friends laughed at Lexi and she knew she couldn't turn the other cheek as she had the last time.

"Aight, pom poms, you got me fucked up."

Keedra stepped in Lexi's face. "Do something, little girl," she dared.

Before anyone knew it, Lexi had grabbed Keedra's weave and slammed her face into a locker several times. "Bitch, you gonna learn about fucking with me," Lexi said as she continued to slam.

"Ladies!" Mr. Johnson said, grabbing Lexi while another teacher grabbed Keedra. During the commotion, Mr. Johnson whispered to Lexi, "Don't worry, I will let Mr. Mackey know she started it," as he got a few feels in. Lexi could care less. She knew Keedra's nose had to be broken and she pulled a few patches of her weave out. She would learn to keep her mouth shut. Getting back in character, Mr. Johnson said, "To the office, ladies!"

Keedra wailed the whole way there, rambling about how Lexi should get expelled for her violence. She was a favorite amongst the staff and she knew she was in the clear. Keedra went to Mr. Mackey's office first and since she was the one bleeding and bruising fast, she sounded convincing with her story that Lexi attacked her out of nowhere for no reason. Mr. Mackey gave her some tissues, told her to call her parents, and assured her immediate action would be taken against Lexi.

Once Keedra walked out the office giving Lexi a dirty look, Lexi entered. She already knew Keedra gave the helpless victim act, so she wasn't going to bullshit. She already knew she had Mr. Johnson on her team, but she was about to have Mr. Mackey eating out of the palm of her hands. After she went in the office and closed the door, she stood there. She wanted to see what would be said first.

"Ms. Savage, seeing how you violently attacked Ms. Tate, I have no choice but to suspend you."

"If you do some research, you'll find out she hit me first and I was defending myself," she said evenly.

"Ms. Savage…"

"Let's cut the bullshit." Lexi jumped on his desk and swung a leg over his head so that she was facing him. "Mr. Mackey, you know Keedra's a bitch. I could care less about getting suspended, expelled, or any of that shit. What I do care about is a bitch lying on me, so since she playing games, I will as well." She grabbed Mr. Mackey's tie and pulled him close to her so she could kiss him. He gave absolutely no resistance and actually loved the way she took control. It just so happened she wore a plaid skirt, white button up shirt with white knees socks, and Mary Janes. The catholic girl school look turned Mr. Mackey on more. She unbuttoned her shirt and put his hands on her breasts. He squeezed them before he sucked her perky nipples. "I can make you feel good. So good. But, what are you going to do for me?" She put her feet on his legs and fingered her pussy.

"There will be no disciplinary actions taken against you?" he said as he watched her.

Lexi started grinding on his desk and moaning softly. "What about Keedra?"

"Ms. Savage..."

Once again, she cut him off by putting her wet fingers in his mouth. He closed his eyes and sucked off her juices. She kissed him as she unbuttoned his shirt, and then she kissed his neck. She went further down and bit his nipples. He undid his pants, anticipating feeling her insides. He opened his desk drawer and pulled out a condom. Lexi noticed that, and made a mental note that he fucked students often in case she needed that information for later. He slid on the condom, pulled her off his desk, and on his lap. He moved her panties to the side and entered her tight, hot wetness. She tightened her muscles and rode him furiously.

"Suspend that bitch and take away her office job."

"Lexi, I can't..." She jumped off his lap, took off the condom, and began sucking his dick. Feeling him ready to explode, she stopped.

"You can't what?" she whispered as she looked at him.

Anyone knew questioning a nigga right at the tip of his nut would get you the answered you needed. "Fine."

"That's what I thought." She opened his drawer, pulled out another condom, and after she rolled it on his dick, she rode him

backwards while he squeezed her tits. "Damn, this dick feel so good, Mr. Mackey. You can have this pussy whenever you want it," Lexi purred. She meant that. Mr. Mackey reminded her of Bank Roll in looks and how he made her feel. She liked fucking him. "You make this pussy feel good, daddy." As she kept whispering, he couldn't hold it any longer. He finally let go of his orgasm while she bounced hard on his dick. Once they were done, she took off her panties and put them in his drawer with the condoms. "I'm glad we could come to a mutual decision."

She pulled the box of baby wipes from her back pack and gave Mr. Mackey a few before she cleaned herself. She sprayed linen scented freshener in the air while her principal got himself together.

"Tell the secretary to write you a pass for class."

"Sure thing, Mr. Mackey." As Lexi left the office, she saw Keedra still waiting for her parents. "Oooo, that don't look too cute. Might wanna get some ice on that, pom poms."

"I'm sure glad I won't be seeing your black ass face for a while," she spat while she covered her swelling eye.

"You sure won't. Enjoy being suspended."

Lexi turned and asked for a pass while Keedra sat there with an open mouth. She knew she wasn't going to be suspended. There was no way Mr. Mackey would betray her as well. They went way back and the way he bent her over his desk and fucked her had her almost in love. She narrowed her eyes. *That bitch just fucked him*, she thought. She was going to get the evidence and blow up everybody's spot.

"We ain't been to Bianca house in a while," Christy said as the girls sat there.

"Slim ain't dicking you down enough?"

"He cool, but I like to fuck different dicks."

Lexi shook her head. "I swear you a fuckin' freak. Come on, let's roll."

When they got to Bianca's, she was sitting in the living room smoking. "Where you been, lil' sis?"

"I been chillin' with this nigga. He cool, but he tryin' to be too boo'd up and shit."

"Girl, ain't nothing wrong with being boo'd up. Shit, I wish I had someone right about now."

"Bitch, hella niggas be at you."

"Niggas wanna fuck, but niggas ain't trying to fuck *with* me."

"Fuck 'em then."

"That's easy to say when you young and don't care about being lonely. Sometimes, I just want someone to hold me at night."

Lexi was about to say something, but someone walked in the door. Christy was already salivating at the thought of new meat. She hadn't seen the stranger before and her insides jumped because she wanted to fuck him. She didn't know what it was, but she liked fucking.

"Lexi, I always miss you when you over here kicking it. Damn, I been looking for you."

"Well, you found me."

"What's up, chocolate?"

"Shit, just been at my aunt's. That's my cousin, Christy."

"Hey," Christy said while smiling.

"He ain't trickin', so put your damn tongue back in your mouth," Lexi said with attitude. She wasn't checking for Devin, but she was tired of Christy ready to fuck any nigga that walked through the door.

"Come ride with me."

"For?"

"Just come on."

Lexi got up. "I'll be back in a few." She jumped in Devin's ride. "What's up?"

"What's up with your sister?"

"You could have asked me that at Bianca's."

"I was just asking. No one has heard from her."

"Well, I'm part of no one."

"Lexi, you know I'm diggin' you, right?"

"Why, wanna see if my pussy feel as good as my sister's?"

"It ain't even like that."

"Oh yea? What's it like then?" Like all niggas, Lexi knew Devin had some sort of hidden agenda.

"I just want a little more of your time. Is that too much to ask for?"

"Time is money, you know that," Lexi replied, unenthused.

The only thing Devin could do was laugh. "I got you." He pulled up at the store. "You want something outta here?"

"Get me a fifth of Henny and some Phillys."

He went in the store and purchased Lexi's items along with what he wanted. They rode back to Bianca's house in silence. Devin knew Lexi was far different than Yesina and he would have to come at her stronger. When he pulled up in front of Bianca's place, he put the car in park.

"Thanks for riding with me. Take my number and hit me up some time."

"Naw, if it's meant to be we'll see each other." Lexi got out the car with her bag and disappeared in Bianca's house, leaving Devin sitting there looking stupid.

"You got round one, chocolate. I got you next time," Devin said to himself as he put the car in drive and rolled off. Although Devin had Yesina at his beck and call, there was something about Lexi that was different. Bank Roll saw it, too, and Devin figured that was why he had Lexi under his thumb. He knew after living with Bank Roll she would be his toughest conquer.

"Drank on me, bitch," Lexi announced when she entered the house. Bianca poured them a glass while Lexi rolled. "Damn, they still in there fucking?"

"Yea, Dutch heard she was over and he back there, too."

"Auntie Liz would flip her wig if she knew Christy was giving up pussy like she is. I bet Stina and Sette the biggest freaks ever. Them hoes already running after some nigga when they need to have a nigga running after them."

"Well, Christy ain't the cutest of the bunch. You know how that goes. Insecure bitches give up more pussy than anybody."

"Christy ain't half bad. If she keep that fucked up hair in braids and lose a few pounds, she'd be cool."

"With at much fucking as she do, she should be a damn bean pole. Sex the best exercise."

"Shit, she eat just as much as she fuck, though."

"What Devin ass talking 'bout?"

Lexi rolled her eyes. "Not a damn thang. Basically, that nigga just want some pussy. You know how niggas is."

"What you gonna do?"

"What I always do. I'll play around and see what's going on. He fucked my sister, so I may or may not fuck him. He cute and all, but I think he just wanna fuck me 'cause I'm Yesina's baby sister."

"I can't call it. That nigga always asking about you, though."

"Girl, you already know niggas jock a bitch harder when they feel they can't have them. It's a game, but I'm the game master."

Bianca laughed. "That nigga don't know what he getting his ass into."

Lexi took a drink. "That's what I'm here for, to show him."

"You a damn fool, that's why I love your ass."

"I ain't even told you the latest drama in my life." Lexi went on to tell Bianca about the situation with Keedra, and the teacher and principal.

Once she was done, Bianca stared at her. "Them muthafuckas at Castlemont have no idea what they dealing with. I bet that Keedra bitch mad as fuck. I ain't never heard of a bitch having a teacher and the principal in her pocket."

"Shit, I'm sure it's been done plenty of times before, that shit was just so on the unda you ain't know about it unless you were the one doing that shit."

Bianca shrugged her shoulders. "True dat."

"I can already tell this will be my last year."

"Lex, I really want you to stay in school and get your diploma. Ain't nothing like walking across that stage."

"How would you know?" she asked, pissed off that Bianca questioned what she wanted to do.

"OK, right now, you hella trippin'. You know I ain't graduate, but there's nothing like doing the work and taking it to completion. You know I'm your bitch and I'm going to always keep it real. You're fucking up if you don't stay there with your aunt and do the right shit. Get out of this ghetto mentality, you know Bank Roll would have wanted that."

"Oh, now you wanna bring Bank Roll in it, huh? Fuck that shit." She walked toward the back and opened the door. "Bitch, get your ass up and come the fuck on. We out."

Christy stopped sucking dick for a moment. "Why?"

"Fuck you. Get left, stupid ass bitch."

Lexi left out of the house, jumped in her car, and left before anyone could blink. An hour later, Christy came from the room with her hair all over the place and her clothes hanging off her.

"Where's Lexi?"

"She left a while ago. You better get your ass home," Bianca told her.

"Umm, can you take me?"

"Bianca was pissed off from the mini argument her and Lexi had. "My car broke down."

Christy looked at Dutch. "Umm, can you...I need to be at 82nd and Outlook."

"I gotta bend some corners and I'm not going that way," he said as he walked out.

Christy looked at the time. It was already midnight. There was no way she was going to make it home before her mother got there. She just hoped Lexi didn't say shit and Elizabeth didn't look in her room. She got herself together and made the walk of shame to the bus stop.

CHAPTER 10

"Hello, class. I will be taking over for Mr. Johnson. My name is Ms. Hope."

"Umm, I sure *hope* I can get close to you," said one of the boys in the class.

"You got that right. If I all my teachers looked like you, I'd be in all my classes," another boy said.

The class laughed and Ms. Hope smirked. "Lame joking will get you boys nowhere. I hope you use better come on lines to the girls your age." The girls in the class were the ones snickering at that point. Ms. Hope went on to talk about what they would be covering in class.

Mr. Johnson had started tripping. Lexi knew he was doing a couple other girls at school, but he was always in her business. He even questioned her about Meech, as if he had the right to. He thought he had access to her pussy 24/7, and when he showed up at her house one night Lexi knew that was enough. She sent an anonymous letter to the principal and the school board stating he was having sexual affairs with students, and when the girls were questioned that were named they were closed mouth until the last girl, Tamika Harris, found out there were other girls in question and got jealous. She told it all, every sordid detail of their affair, and when the previous girls were questioned again they ended up breaking and confessing as well. Lexi didn't expect his replacement to be the gorgeous Ms. Hope. She knew she would pick up a few things about grace and poise from her.

She looked so beautiful and elegant to Lexi. She had on a peach pantsuit with a white blouse and white pumps. Her hair was rolled in a tight bun and her makeup was flawless. She looked to be in her late twenties, early thirties, but Lexi figured she was in her forties. She liked her style. Over the weeks, she noticed how she kept her class together with a no nonsense attitude. All the young niggas wanted her, and Lexi found herself to be attracted to her as well.

Walking to the car, Lexi noticed Christy drooling over some nigga she hadn't seen before. "Who that?" she asked.

"That's Robert. His momma sent him down south last year with their peoples because he was getting in these streets. I guess he came back home."

Lexi looked him over. "He kinda cute," she said. He wore dark blue Levis and a white shirt with white K-Swiss.

"He fuck with this bitch named Tanya." Christy looked at him again. "There her punk ass go now."

Lexi turned up her nose as Tanya walked up on Robert and gave him a peck on the cheek. "She look like a church girl. Wait, don't she go to y'all church?" Lexi remembered seeing her a few times before.

"Yea. She teach the kids' Sunday School."

Lexi shook her head. "You know she ain't giving up pussy, go on and give him what he need."

"My momma would kill me. Everybody know they gonna get married and be together forever."

"Who says she has to know?" Christy's face was filled with doubt. "I'll take care of it."

The next day, Lexi saw Robert in the hall. "Hey, you. Come here."

Robert looked around. He gave a cocky smile as he walked toward Lexi. He figured she was one of the many girls that swooned over him. He leaned against a locker when he got close to her. "What's up, sexy chocolate?"

Lexi smacked her lips. "Boy, please. I got some hook up for you. You know my cousin, Christy?"

"Christy Savage? That's your cousin?"

"The one and only. Anyways, if you ain't a whipped lil' pussy, come through the house around seven." Lexi knew challenging manhood pissed niggas off. Plus, it was free pussy in the package as well.

Robert shrugged his shoulders. "Aight."

At around ten after seven, there was a knock at the door. Christy jumped to get it. "Bitch, sit down. That nigga late, make his ass wait."

"He may leave."

"He won't," Lexi said confidently. She waited another moment, and then slowly walked to the door while Christy sat on pins and needles. She swung the door open. "Niggas that want some pussy ain't late," she stated boldly.

"Who said I wanted pussy?"

"You're here, right?" Lexi answered sassily.

She stepped to the side and let Robert in. Niggas were so easy. Christy sat there looking like she had an orgasm just having him in her house. He was pretty cute, but Christy always acted so desperate.

"What's up, Christy?" Robert said with a smile as he smoothly sat down next to her.

"Umm…nothing…what's up?"

Lexi rolled her eyes and shook her head. She couldn't understand why that girl was so pathetic.

"So, you been diggin' a brotha, huh?"

"Umm, yea." She smiled. She felt confident in cut off sweats and a t-shirt. The shirt was loose enough to hide her stomach and the shorts fit just right, showing her thick legs.

Robert checked her out. He would have preferred if Lexi had been trying to push up on him, but pussy was all the same. Tanya said she wasn't giving it up until they got married and he had to get it from somewhere. He rubbed Christy's leg and she giggled.

"Imma leave y'all alone. I'll be back later, Christy." Lexi left, and Christy wasted no time getting down to business.

Lexi pulled up to Bianca's apartment. "Hey, girl. What you doing here?"

"I left Christy at home to fuck some nigga she all on."

"Who dick ain't she on?"

"Tell me about it. He pretty cute, though. Some church nigga that's fucking with some church girl."

"That girl need to find someone that just wanna fuck with her."

"I don't know, she think fucking is love or something. Hell, I really don't know what she think." Bianca fired up a blunt and after she hit it, she passed it to Lexi. "Devin been around?"

"He came through earlier. He asked about you."

"What that nigga want with me for real?"

"For the first time, I can't call it. He may really be digging you, may wanna be the nigga got fucked both the Savage sisters, or he could simply wanna have what Bank Roll had," she answered with a shrug. Although the last time they saw each other there was some friction, it was squashed before they saw each other again.

"He got his paper up? Seem like I don't know shit about none of these niggas no more. I need to keep my ears to the streets better than I do."

"He doing cool."

"Who he fucking?"

"He got a baby with Slap."

"Get the fuck outta here." Slap was two years older than Lexi. Her and Yesina had been friends at one point. They called her Slap because she always started her fights by slapping the piss out of a bitch. "When Slap had a baby?"

Bianca laughed. "You was way far up Bank Roll's ass, huh? She had the baby before Devin went to jail."

"What was my ass doing? I don't remember none of that shit."

"That's because you was in school, doing homework, or on some vacation with ya man."

Lexi picked up her cup and took a swig. "Man, I had so much fun with him. He showed me a whole new life. How many bitches can say they been to half the places I've been and I ain't even legal yet? I remember when we went to that fight in Vegas. I was drinking and gambling like my ass was grown."

"Yea, you've done it up."

"I can't live like this. I love Auntie Lizzie to death, but I can't live a life full of rules."

"Rules can be good. It's not always good to wild out and be living on the edge. At least try to finish up school, you know Bank Roll wanted that more than anything." Bianca knew it was a dead conversation, but she felt like she had to say it. She owed Bank Roll that.

"He's not here anymore, so it doesn't matter."

"If you leave, then what?"

"Imma live life my way. I'm not meant to be pinned in the house doing some crazy bullshit. Yea, I do like school and shit, but that was more for Bank Roll." Lexi looked at Bianca. "Mind if I crash here? You know I got you."

"I really want you to stay in school and live a different life 'cause this street life ain't no joke, but you know you always welcome here." Bianca couldn't say no to Lexi. If she wasn't at Elizabeth's house, she at least wanted Lexi to be around someone who had her back.

"Who's to say which life is right? I know Auntie Lizzie provides a really nice life, but all her daughters are wild. Shit, give it a few years and I bet them granddaughters of hers gonna be just as wild."

"You probably right about that."

"I'm still thinking about it, but you know me, my mind is pretty made up."

"Well, whenever you're ready, come on over."

Lexi gave Bianca a hug. "We gonna run this muthafucka."

"You got that right."

"Imma get up outta here. I'm going to try to at least finish the school year, but who knows. I do have fun with my boy toys there, though. I'll keep you updated."

"You a mess. What them niggas like at the Castle?"

"You know I ain't checking for some lil' young niggas. There's a few cute boys and they be doing they thing, but unless a nigga on Bank Roll level, he can't do shit for me but pass time."

"I heard that. What's up with that Meech nigga?"

"I'm tired of him. It was so easy to get that nigga caught up. Nigga be trying to act like they hard and running shit, but don't be running nothing but they mouth."

"That's niggas everywhere."

"Who you telling?"

"Be easy out there, girl."

CHAPTER 11

Lexi had just come from fucking the principal and had her hall pass to get in Ms. Hope's class. Mr. Mackey had no money to splurge on her because he barely made enough to take care of himself, but there were perks with fucking the principal and she loved the way he fucked her.

When she walked in class, Ms. Hope looked over the note and frowned at Lexi. Lexi rolled her eyes and took her seat. The rest of the period, she paid no attention to Ms. Hope or what she taught. She knew she could leave at any time, and she was ready to bounce. She got tired of Christina and Chrisette visiting and getting on her nerves, but she did find the stories of Drama and Diva funny. From what she heard, Drama always got into something, and it wasn't always something good. Diva was more laid back, but she did her fair share of wilding out as well.

As the bell rang for class to end, Ms. Hope stopped Lexi from leaving. "I'd like to speak with you, Ms. Savage." Lexi stopped in her tracks and turned around. "Have a seat," she said, waving toward one of the desks. When the door was closed and only the two of them were in the class, Ms. Hope spoke again. "You seem to be popular with the male teachers here."

"What's it to you?" Lexi said dismissively.

"Hmm, you're a bad little thing, huh?"

Lexi rolled her eyes. "What do you want?"

Ms. Hope leaned down low. Lexi could smell her intoxicating perfume. The heat she generated made Lexi feel

something. She rubbed the length of Lexi's chocolate arm, leaving a trail of raised hairs. "I want you," she whispered.

Lexi froze. It was the first time she had been at a lost for words. "I don't fuck women," Lexi said harshly, and then walked out of the room.

Ms. Hope smiled. "Not yet," she whispered as she watched Lexi's fat ass bounce out of the room.

"I ain't get my period," Christy said to Lexi.

Lexi shook her head. "Who you been letting hit it raw?" Christy was quiet. "Bitch, you been letting all them niggas nut all in you?"

"No...I...well..."

"You stupid."

"Most of the time they pull out before they nut," she said quietly.

"Shit, do you even have an idea who baby it is?"

"I think Robert 'cause he the only one that nut in me all the time."

"Why your ass ain't on the pill?"

"I forget to take 'em most of the time."

"Why don't you make them niggas strap up? You don't know what type of shit a nigga got crawling up his dick."

"They say they be clean. And Robert, he go to my church. I'm sure he don't have nothing."

Lexi sighed. "He don't have nothing, but now you pregnant. What you gonna do? Aunt Lizzie will kick your ass."

"I don't know. Imma talk to Robert."

"Good luck with that. You think he gonna leave perfect Tanya for you? A nigga wife up the square girl and fuck the sluts."

"He said he love me."

Lexi rolled her eyes. "Niggas tell every bitch they love 'em. Don't tell me you believe that shit."

"He said he gonna leave her and be with me."

"You have absolutely no game."

Christy began to tear up. She loved Robert and wanted him to leave Tanya for her. She was happy to be pregnant. She had

longed for someone all of her own to love, and there was no way Robert would deny her. "It's gonna be cool, watch."

The talk hadn't gone the way Christy expected. She wanted Robert to say he'd leave Tanya and marry her so they could raise their child. Instead, he pulled out some money and told her to take care of it. She thought against it, but what if it wasn't Robert's in the end? What would her mother do finding out she was pregnant at seventeen. Both her sisters had babies when they were teens, but it was always different for her. She didn't go to the clinic and didn't talk to Lexi any more about it. She went back and forth on the situation and about three weeks later, she finally made an appointment to get an abortion.

When the procedure was done, she felt so guilty. She cried and cried. Deep inside, she wanted that baby. She wanted to love it like her mother never loved her. She knew she would never leave the baby on someone's doorstep to never return. She wanted to be everything to her baby that her real mother hadn't been to her, but she didn't get the chance and she regretted it.

Robert never came by after she told him she was pregnant and in church he acted as if she didn't exist. She despised the way him and Tanya sat up in church as everyone looked at them as if God Himself had come down and put them together. She hated them, and she knew one day she would have some sort of revenge for the baby she had to kill.

CHAPTER 12

Lexi was bored with church, school, Auntie Lizzie, and everything else she could think of. She missed her sister and wondered where she was. Although she hung out with Bianca as much as she could, she needed more excitement in her life.

She dragged her feet as she went to Ms. Hope's class. She had been ditching it since she had made her feel uncomfortable. Ms. Hope told her to stay afterwards when the bell rang for class to end.

"Why you stay on my case?" Lexi asked as the students left.

"You missed an important test."

"Mr. Mackey said it's cool for me to make up anything I miss on my free period," Lexi said with an attitude.

"Seems like Mr. Mackey has taken quite a liking to you." Lexi rolled her eyes. "I've noticed you miss class a lot and stay in Mr. Mackey's office, but your grades are excellent. How does that happen?" Again, Ms. Hope circled Lexi like prey.

"You're going to make me late for class."

Ms. Hope smiled. "Since when did you care about class or being late?"

She ran her manicured nails down Lexi's arm. She could feel her quiver. Lexi hadn't even noticed that the door had been closed and locked. She slightly rubbed Lexi's thigh, making her open them without thought. She lightly licked Lexi's lips, making Lexi close her eyes and savor her touch. Slowly, she inched up her

black skirt to discover she wasn't wearing panties. She fingered Lexi's moistness.

"I just love sweet, chocolate girls like you. I remember when I was your age, I was so hot and wanted to fuck all the time," Ms. Hope whispered. "What about you, Lexi? Do you have that itch right about," she stuck her finger deeper inside Lexi, "here?"

All Lexi could do was moan. She didn't know what Ms. Hope was doing to her, but it was something she had never experience, not even with Bank Roll. Ms. Hope continued to finger her, making her juices flow freely. "I bet it tastes so sweet," Ms. Hope whispered in Lexi's ear after she kissed her neck. Lexi couldn't respond. She was caught up in her seduction. Then, Ms. Hope got on her knees and began to taste Lexi. She leaned back in the small desk and tried to give Ms. Hope full access to her pussy. Her tongue was so soft and skillful. Lexi thought of Bank Roll. He had taught her everything, but he didn't teach her how to keep her guard up from a woman.

After that day, Lexi was gone. She was always in Ms. Hope's class bright and early. She begged to taste her, but Ms. Hope wouldn't let her. She did, however, keep Lexi right where she wanted her. She wanted to feel those pretty lips taste her nectar, but she had to tame Ms. Lexi Savage. Ms. Hope was the female counterpart of her work place. As Mr. Mackey and Mr. Johnson loved the young girls, and she loved the young girls and boys. They were always so ready and willing. The boys were always hard and ready to go. They were able to be taught to do the things she loved and they learned so fast. She didn't mess with many young girls because they got too caught up, but she couldn't help herself sometimes. Their tight bodies and firm breasts turned her on. Being a teacher was like working in a candy store every day. She had to be careful with the girls because they were way clingier than the boys. The boys were just happy to fuck the hot teacher. She had to make sure she picked the right ones. The ones that wouldn't blab and let all the business be known. So far, they had all been on point.

A week and three mind blowing sessions later, Ms. Hope figured it was time. She was so glad her free period was the one after the class Lexi had with her. She sat on her desk with her legs

crossed as Lexi sat in hers. She slowly unbuttoned her shirt and unclasped her bra, and then she slowly beckoned for Lexi with her finger.

Lexi's mouth watered at the thought of finally having a taste. She walked toward Ms. Hope as if she was hypnotized. She eagerly put a nipple in her mouth and sucked away. The way Ms. Hope softly purred turned Lexi on more. She was dizzy under her spell. Her heart beat so fast, she thought it would beat out of her chest. She took her time and kissed Ms. Hope slowly and softly. She wanted her to know how much she wanted it. As she made her way down her stomach to her pierced navel, her insides went wild as she thought of finally tasting her. Ms. Hope didn't let up. She laid back on the desk and opened her legs, exposing her neatly trimmed pussy. Lexi took a deep breath, and then began to lick her clit that was so hard. She stuck her fingers inside as Ms. Hope had done so many times to her. She was so sweet and so wet. Lexi was taken into another world when she came from just the thought of making Ms. Hope cum. When Ms. Hope did cum, it was a wrap. Lexi had written a check she couldn't cash.

***

It had been two months since Lexi had been blown away by her sexy teacher. Ms. Hope had taught Lexi womanly things that Bank Roll would have never been able to show her. She was almost like the mother she never had and she was in love. From spending countless nights laid up in Ms. Hope's arms, Lexi found out she was forty one and had never been married or had kids. Her name was Nina, but it turned her on when Lexi called her Ms. Hope. She had her first experience with a girl when she was only ten. Vanessa, her best friend, was spending the weekend at her house as she often did. They were both curious about sex and had been having feelings they hadn't felt before. They began talking about things and wanted to practice kissing for when they had a first kiss from a boy. That kiss led to them fondling each other, exploring each other's body.

Nina felt comfortable because she knew the spots that throbbed on her young body, so she knew exactly what to do to Vanessa's body, and vice versa. They loved spending the night

with each other because when the lights went off, they sexed each other up like young lovers.

Things changed when they got to the sixth grade. Nina filled out faster than Vanessa, having a round butt and perky tits that the boys loved. She loved the things she did with Vanessa, but she was curious to find out how it would be to have sex with a boy. Gary Johnson was the lucky one that was going to pop her cherry. They often met behind the bleachers at school to kiss while he explored her body. Gary was in the eighth grade and was popular. He had just started having sex himself, but once he got a feel of busting a nut in a pussy he wanted to do it all the time. He had his eye on Nina because she was young and he knew she was a virgin. She had bouncy titties, pretty lips, and he wanted to bust her hole wide open.

One weekend, Nina's parents went out of town. She told them she was going to Vanessa's house, but she stayed home so Gary could come over and fuck her. Once she got that dick in her, it was a done deal. She found herself fucking Gary every chance she got, leaving Vanessa jealous while Nina told her all the sordid details of their sexual encounters. Vanessa wanted to feel a dick, too. She wanted her girlfriend back so they could kiss and rub each other, and lick each other's clit. As she listened to Nina tell her what had gone on between her and Gary, she laid in bed and rubbed her clit, wishing she was there with them while they were fucking.

After a while, Nina missed Vanessa as well. She hadn't spent the night in almost a month so Nina asked her over. When the lights went out in the house the girls were up to their usual, but it didn't feel right to Nina. She really enjoyed Vanessa, but she really enjoyed Gary and wanted him there.

She got on top of Vanessa and grinded on her as she kissed her. "I got an idea," she whispered.

"What's up?"

"You ready to get your cherry popped?"

"What you mean?"

"I'm going to call Gary over so we all can do it."

Vanessa was excited. She so wanted to feel the way Nina had felt. The way she described the feeling of the hard dick going

in and out of her pussy made Vanessa so hot and bothered, she would make herself cum several times a night. Gary was so fine, too. He was five feet seven with wavy hair. He was a peanut butter color with the prettiest brown eyes. He had a deep voice like a grown man, and he didn't have pimples like most of the boys at school.

Nina picked up the phone and called Gary. When they weren't having sex they made sure all the other phones in the house was unplugged or the ringer off so they could call each other. Gary knew Vanessa was spending the night, so he didn't expect Nina to call and didn't go through their ritual. When his mother picked up the phone, Nina quickly hung up.

"Shit, his momma answered. We may not be able to make it happen tonight."

Vanessa was disappointed, but tried not to show it. She put her arm around Nina and pulled her close. They were about to start kissing again when the phone rang. Nina answered before the first ring finished.

"Gary?" she whispered.

"Yea, you just called?"

"Yea, can you sneak out and come over?"

"I thought Vanessa was spending the night?"

"She is, but I still wanna see you. Just come on."

"OK. The phone woke up my momma and she's in the kitchen, but she'll be back in bed soon and I'll be over."

"My window will be open, just come in."

Gary lay still in his bed as he listened to the sounds in his home. His mother finally had left the kitchen, went to the restroom, and then back to bed. He knew she would be snoring in no time. He waited ten minutes, which seemed more like ten hours, and then crept out of his bed, out of his window, and sprinted the two blocks to Nina's house. Her window was cracked just as promised, and he slipped in.

He loved having sex with Nina. She was so open and freaky, unlike the other girls. Nina had even sucked his dick, something no one had done and in turn, he licked her middle as she had requested. He was hesitant at first, but once he saw the way she went crazy he wanted to lick it more. They did all kinds of

things and he didn't want to have sex with anyone but Nina. Until, he saw Vanessa naked in the bed with Nina.

"What are you doing?" He was caught off guard and his voice was louder than it should have been.

"Shhhh! Are you crazy?" Gary stood there frozen. Never in a million years did he think he would see the sight before him. His dick instantly got hard. Nina got up, walked over to him, and kissed him. "Vanessa needs her cherry to be popped," she said confidently. "I told her how good you feel. Can you make her feel good, too?"

Gary cleared his throat. "Umm, are you sure?"

Nina began stroking his dick. "I know you got more than enough to go around. So, will you?" Gary shrugged his shoulders. "I'm going to get her ready. I'm going to bend over my bed so you can give it to me from behind." He simply nodded his head.

Nina bent over and began tasting Vanessa. Gary's mind was blown. It all made sense to him at that moment. He knew Nina and Vanessa were best friends, and he often thought he saw little gestures between them that was more than friends. When Vanessa seemed to instantly hate him when he started fucking Nina, he thought she was just jealous but he never figured she was jealous because he had stolen her lover.

Nina licked Vanessa, sticking her fingers in her tight hole. She knew having both of them together would be the best feeling in the world. Not only did she have Gary stroking her, she had her face buried between her girlfriend's legs and it was the shit. When Vanessa had an orgasm that made her pussy sloppy wet, Nina moved out of the way and motioned for Gary to enter her. He laid on Vanessa and kissed her, surprised to taste Nina's pussy on her lips. He slowly worked his way inside of her while he kissed Nina, tasting Vanessa's juices on her lips. They went back and forth almost all night, and finally Gary pulled himself away from the freaky experience and rushed home to sneak in his window.

After that night, the three often got together until Vanessa's parents got divorced and she moved to the east coast with her mother. Shortly after that, Gary moved to southern California with his parents and Nina was left alone. She was stuck in a sexual frenzy, but she knew what to do to get her peers to give her what

she wanted. It was when she fucked her first teacher that she decided she would be a teacher herself and have access to her heart's desires.

Lexi never thought she would make it to the end of the school year, but lusting after Ms. Hope kept her there. She was glad Meech had gone to jail because with him living a few blocks away from her he was a borderline stalker. He popped up at lunch, after school, or anytime at Lexi's house. She was glad he didn't know where Bianca stayed or he would have popped up there as well. She hadn't been interested in him or Mr. Mackey anymore, the only person on her mind was Ms. Hope. She told Lexi she loved her and the way she made Lexi feel, she believed her. There had been several men that had professed their love, but that was just words to Lexi. She knew it was a game that all niggas played. She felt like the words from Ms. Hope were pure because her touch was something definitely different. The way she held her with care and whispered in Lexi's ear, there was no way she could be deceiving. She even slipped cards and small notes in Lexi's locker, making her fall hard.

Ms. Hope had moved it from her classroom to her home and although she hadn't asked Lexi to drop by, she had to have a taste. After knocking on the door with no answer, she looked through the window. She knew Ms. Hope was home because her car was there. What she saw was nothing she had seen before. Ms. Hope was laid out on her couch getting her pussy ate by a nigga Lexi had seen around school while he was getting fucked by another nigga. Lexi looked harder and noticed him to be someone named Rico. It was that moment she got her shit together and got over Ms. Hope, but she didn't get over her love for pussy. When it was all said and done, it made Lexi an even badder bitch without her even knowing. She got back in ice heart mode and trusted no one. She convinced herself that anyone that wanted to fuck wanted just that, and she was sure love of any kind didn't exist. Like Bank Roll, Lexi kept a picture of her and Ms. Hope to remind her that love was nothing more than a four letter word that meant shit.

CHAPTER 13

Not wanting to go back to school and look in Ms. Hope's deceiving face, Lexi packed her shit and left in the middle of the night. She left Elizabeth a note thanking her for her hospitality and told her it was time for her to go. She knew her aunt would worry, but she knew Elizabeth would understand Lexi was from the streets and thrived being in that lifestyle. She tried to square up, but it fucked her up and took her off her game. She felt so foolish for falling in love and putting herself in a position to feel like she did.

After riding around for a while, at one in the morning she pulled up to Bianca's apartment. Even though it was a Tuesday night there seemed to be a party going because there was a host of people hanging out and chilling. The door wasn't locked, so Lexi turned the knob and walked in with her belongings.

"Finally made that move, huh?"

"Yea, it was time."

"That bitch got you twisted, didn't she?"

Lexi sighed. "Something like that."

"Well, come make a drink and blow something. Ain't nothing like a woman's touch and that shit can blow ya mind, but you will get it together."

"Let's go to Vegas this weekend," Lexi suggested, wanting to get away.

"You know I'm with it. Hell, let's leave tomorrow."

"That's even better. I just need to get away."

Bianca sat down on the couch next to Lexi. "Look, bitch, remember when you told me to help keep you in check?"

"Yea."

"Well, dammit, you outta check right now. I know pussy is some good shit, but get it together. A woman's touch is so different from a man's, and women know what women like. They are soft and whisper hella sweet shit. If you not aware you will be fucked over. What you think Bank Roll would say right now?"

"I know, and you right. That shit just blew my mind, though. I mean, real talk, she made me feel better than Bank Roll ever did."

"Snap outta la la land. Get it together 'cause we 'bout to go to Vegas and get some niggas for their money."

Getting over on niggas always made Lexi perk up. "You right. But tonight, let's get our party on."

They drank, partied, and bullshitted until the sun came up. The next afternoon, both girls were up and ready to go. Bianca had gotten a dopefiend rental from Bootsie, who lived up the street. As they were putting their bags in the car, Christy walked up.

"Where y'all going?"

"Somewhere you can't," Lexi answered.

"We going to Vegas, sweetie."

"You ain't old enough for Vegas," Christy said to Lexi.

"Bitch, I'm old enough for whatever I wanna do."

"Why you leave? Momma worried."

"Auntie Lizze knew it wouldn't last long. I'm not fit for y'all world. You got plenty of contacts to keep you dicked up, don't worry."

"It ain't about...dick ain't...you trippin'," Christy said with a nervous laugh.

"The bitch always stuttering when she lying. She know she worried about if she gonna be cut outta dick."

She looked meekly at Bianca. "Can I still come over sometimes?"

Bianca could do nothing but laugh. "Sure. You know I got an open door policy. If I'm home, it's all good."

"How long y'all gonna be gone?"

"Till we get back," Lexi snapped.

"I'll hit you up. Don't worry about Ms. Evil over there."

"Well, call momma when you can."

Lexi rolled her eyes and got in the passenger seat. She knew she was going to have to cut off that side of her Savage family in order to do what she needed to do in life. Bianca got in the car and they drove off with Christy standing there watching them. She knew it would be the last time she saw either of them for a while.

"Stop by the store so we can get some drank."

"I'm already on it. I got an ounce from Scrape this morning while you was still passed out."

"My kind of talk."

They stopped at the store, prepared their drinks and blunts, and jumped on the freeway. The ride seemed like nothing as the girls laughed and acted a fool the whole way. There were times they flashed drivers and got some laughs in. Vegas' bright lights and energy welcomed the two with opened arms.

"What we getting into first?" Lexi asked, ready to get into everything.

"Let's find a room so we can shower and change."

"Sounds like a plan. When I came with Bank Roll, we always stayed at the Caesars."

"Caesars it is then."

"I wonder if Sin out here somewhere," Lexi said more to herself. She hadn't seen her sister in a while and she wondered if she was dead or alive.

"Where ever she at, I'm sure she cool," Bianca responded, sensing the worry in Lexi's demeanor.

"I sure hope so. Last time I saw her it definitely wasn't a good picture. She got too much game to let a nigga treat her fucked up."

"I agree. Y'all are Savages, she won't be down for long. I bet she already making it do what it do."

"Yea," was all Lexi responded with as the pulled up to their hotel of choice.

They paid valet and went in to check into a room. Lexi went in her stash and paid for a week. She wasn't sure how long they would be there, but she figured a week was a good start. The

girls went into their plush two bedroom suite and indulged in long, hot showers. They turned on the stereo in the living room, and sang and danced while they got dressed in their rooms.

"Damn, this a nice fucking room," Bianca said as she walked around.

"Bank Roll got me spoiled to big shit. I like that dress, girl."

Lexi checked Bianca out. She had on a short, electric blue dress that tied around the neck, and it hugged every curve on her body. Her heels were vicious, giving her shapely legs length and definition. Her long singles hung down her back with soft curls dangling from a few random braids.

"You looking pretty fly yourself."

Lexi had on a white dress that was just as clingy as Bianca's and it was strapless. She had on silver stilettos with silver earrings, and her fresh wrap was combed down and framed her chocolate face.

"Let's hit the strip and see what kind of trouble we can get into," Lexi suggested.

They headed out, getting stares and whistles as they made their way downstairs and through the lobby. When the night air hit them, they felt more invigorated and ready to conquer the world, or at least Vegas. They bounced in and out of casinos, hanging out with the high rollers and betting their money. They tossed back drink after drink, and smoked with other niggas out enjoying Vegas life.

Lexi spotted a strip club having amateur night. "Girl, let's go check them out," she said with her arm intertwined in Bianca's, pulling her in the club.

They ordered a drink soon as they stepped in and found a spot to watch what the girls had to offer. Lexi rolled her eyes. "These bitches hella whack. I'm about to show them how it's s'posed to be done."

Bianca laughed. "I knew Bank Roll ain't have that pole in the house for nothing."

"Damn skippy."

Lexi walked toward the guy that put the ladies on the list that wanted to show their goods. She had another drink with

Bianca, and when her name was called she confidently walked to the stage like she owned the entire place. Her penetrating eyes seemed to have touched every horny bastard in the building. She seductively shook and gyrated to the music until she was down to her silver thong. The club went wild, and once her dance was over the owner offered her a job. He wanted her on his team.

"I just wanted to test the waters. Who knows, maybe I'll be back." Lexi said as she batted her eyelashes and flirted.

"I sure hope so. Even if you don't want to dance, take my card so I can take you to lunch."

"OK, daddy." Lexi loved calling men daddy. She knew it turned them on, and gave them some sense of power and authority.

They left the strip club and walked into another casino to gamble with Lexi's earnings. They rolled dice and had won the room money back. They played roulette and won enough money to stay another month in Vegas without touching any of the money they had brought with them.

"You must be a good luck charm because everything we touch is hot!" Bianca said.

"I think both of you ladies are good luck charms."

The girls turned around and pretended not to be star struck. The fine man that had just spoken to them was none other than up and coming rapper Twin Star. He chose the name because he had a twin brother that moved down south to go to school and pursue a degree in entertainment law. They both were stars in their own right, and they were fine. They were identical, standing at five feet eleven with deep cocoa skin. They had dark brown eyes and dimples set on the right side of their face. The only way to tell them apart was Twin Star wore fashionable braids and a mouth full of gold while Jeffrey Brown opted for a low cut fade and no gold to keep his business look professional.

"We are," Lexi answered and turned around to throw the dice. Bianca followed up with a smirk as she blew on the dice Lexi was about to throw.

"Y'all need to kick it with me tonight." Lexi paid him no mind as she hit seven and collected her winnings. "You know how many bitches would die for an opportunity like this?" he asked, offended that they didn't even give him a response.

Lexi waved him off. "Go find them bitches you speak of then. *Ladies* don't give a fuck about you."

Twin Star took a step back and looked at them. "This is a mistake you're going to regret."

Lexi shrugged her shoulders and paid him no attention. When he walked off, Bianca finally spoke. "Damn, bitch, how can I be like you?"

"You know how the game go. That nigga wanna fuck with us ten times more now. Maybe we'll bump into him later, if not, it wasn't meant to be."

"I trust you. But damn, Twin Star? I don't know if I would have been able to wave him off so easily."

They played dice a little more, taking in the free drinks and flirting like no tomorrow. They ended up going in the first club they saw and paid to be in VIP. They popped bottles and danced the night away. Bianca slightly tapped Lexi and whispered to her to look toward the left. Two tables over was none other than Twin Star and his entourage.

"It must be meant to be, but that nigga will come to us. You know the rules, don't beg for no dick."

They popped a bottle of Moet and began sipping. Ironically, the club played Twin Star's song, and he got up and began lip synching to it with a gang of groupies surrounding him. Lexi and Bianca danced with each other, oblivious to anyone around them. They passed the bottle of Moet to each other, showing every bit of their hood mentality as they drank straight from the bottle. Twin Star spotted them and watched for a while. He wanted them so bad he thought his dick would explode. They were top notch bitches, and he knew they weren't the average groupies. They had secured a private table for themselves and had popped at least three bottles of Moet since he had noticed them. He almost felt ashamed for coming at them the way he had earlier. He gave it another hour to make sure they weren't the girls of some ball player or rapper, and seeing them only with each other the entire night, he finally decided to make his move.

"Well, well, we meet again, ladies."

"We do," Lexi responded, giving him a cold once over.

"So, what y'all ladies do? You must be a stylist to the stars or some PR chicks." He knew they weren't the average hood chicks because they were dressed in name brands and didn't look like they hurt for a dime. He could sniff women from a mile away that had saved up their entire welfare check for an outfit from the ones that lived liked that on a daily.

"We handle our own, that's what we do," Lexi shot back curtly.

"Whoa, lil' momma, I'm just tryin to get to know two lovely ladies," Twin Star responded with his hands in the air.

"Don't mind my girl, she can be pretty straight up with no chaser at times," Bianca added, trying to ease the tension. Lexi was always hardcore, and at times Bianca felt it was too much.

"It's cool. Better than the gold digging groupies that stay in my face." The waitress came over to ask if anyone needed anything. "Bring three bottles of Moet over here and send two bottles to the table over there," Twin Star said, pointing to the table he was previously at.

"What you doing out here? Business or pleasure?" Bianca asked.

"I got a show tomorrow night. I would love it if you ladies were my special guests."

"What do we get as special guests?" Lexi looked around. "As you can see, we can start a party by ourselves and have a damn good time doing it."

"You right, lil' momma. You get a private table, unlimited drinks and appetizers, and front of the line privilege no matter what time you arrive."

"Sounds like a deal to me." Lexi gave Twin Star a wink and gave him their name for the guest list. "Don't play me or I will blow your spot up and you can kiss your little career goodbye."

He let out a small laugh. "Damn, you go hard."

"I'm a town bitch, daddy, we do nothing but go hard."

"I respect that." Twin Star kissed her hand, Bianca's, and walked back to his table.

"I heard that nigga got a big dick," Bianca told Lexi.

"I've heard that, too. We gonna turn that nigga out after his performance tomorrow and you gonna be his bitch. He got some

lyrics, so I'm sure he'll make a lil' dough and whatever he make you make sure he spending that shit on you."

"I got that. Bank Roll trained me right."

CHAPTER 14

It was the next night and the girls were in their suite getting ready for their night. They took showers, and the room smelled fresh and clean. Room service brought appetizers and two bottles of champagne to get the party started. Lexi chose a yellow lace dress with a yellow thong and yellow bra underneath. She had on strappy yellow stilettos and had her hair done in Shirley Temple curls. She sprayed on her signature Chanel No. 5 and popped open a bottle.

"Here's to starting a new life," Lexi said.

"Damn right," Bianca responded, taking a big swig after Lexi.

Bianca wore gold shorts with a gold top that tied around her neck with cleavage spilling for days. She had on black stilettos and her hair in two high ponytails, giving her an innocent look. She wore Gucci perfume, her favorite scent since she had first smelled it.

"We about to run this town tonight. I just want to have a good fucking time."

"I'm with that."

They finished the two bottles and headed out. They gambled a little and bullshitted with old men with old money. They had collected a few numbers as well as key cards. They had promising prospects, but the night was still young.

"We hitting up Twin Star party tonight?"

"Hell yea, we are. We 'bout to pop the most expensive bottles in that bitch and we going do it liver than it's ever been done. We ain't going early, though. We going on our time."

"You hella ruthless."

Lexi arched and eyebrow. "That's how I was bred, baby."

"You's a cold bitch, but you know that's why I love you."

"I know." Lexi stuck out her tongue at Bianca and downed the shot of Hennessy that was in front of her.

About two hours later, they finally went to the club where Twin Star performed. The line was around the corner and everybody looked impatient. From the mumbles, they had been in line for a while because the club was already at full capacity. The girls walked confidently to the front of the line and gave their names. With no hesitation, they were let in the club and someone inside escorted them to their awaiting VIP table. There were already various bottles waiting for them and they wasted no time getting the party started. They got dirty stares and had bitches rolling their eyes, but that meant nothing to them. They ignored the bullshit and did their thing in their own world.

When they were good and tipsy, Twin Star appeared on the stage and started the show. The girls danced with each other and sang the lyrics to his songs. Before he started the third song, he spoke to the audience, thanking them for their support. He ended his speech when he looked at the table he had waiting for Lexi and Bianca. When he saw them, he smiled.

"My special guests are here and I want you fine ladies to join me on stage.

Lexi and Bianca looked at each other and shrugged. "Let's go, bitch," Bianca said.

Lexi wasted no time. She tried to be hard, but she was taken back to that eleven year old girl that wanted to be a rapper's dancer, shaking her ass on stage and having niggas lusting after her.

They made their way to the stage, and Twin Star did his famous song where he talked about how freaky he was and what he would do to the right one. He gave the girls a personal lap dance, and some would have sworn they were actually fucking on stage the way he moved his body in synch with theirs. They looked like

they had practiced the seemingly live sex show for hours. When the song was over both girls were hot and bothered, and the unsaid agreement between the two was that they were going to kick it with him the rest of the night.

After the show they left with Twin Star and his entourage, and had a mini party in the limo. They drove around drinking and smoking, then Twin Star passed around an old school album cover with lines of coke on it. The girls looked at each other and figured what the hell. They were ready for whatever. They both sniffed a line and allowed the drug to work its magic. By the time they arrived at Twin Star's suite, there was a completely different party going on. His suite made theirs look like they paid for it with bubble gum money. His living room looked to be the size their entire suite was and the furnishing was top of the line.

The girls mixed and mingled, going around talking shit as they stole the show. There were plenty of top notch bitches and seasoned gold diggers there, but Lexi and Bianca definitely held their own. One of the guys in Twin Star's entourage tried to talk to Lexi. She gave him small talk and politely excused herself. The same thing happened when another member of the entourage tried to talk to Bianca. The girls flirted lightly, but let it be known they were just there to have fun. Besides, their eyes were on the prize. They had something special in store for Twin Star, and they played their moves like a chess game to get him where they wanted him. They enjoyed the night fully, making sure they were nowhere in Twin Star's presence the entire time. When they saw the sun coming up, Lexi elbowed Bianca so they could leave.

"It's been a long night. I ain't partied like this in a long time."

"I don't think I've partied like this ever. I've had a lot of fun with Bank Roll, but that was different."

"I feel you. Let's see what else we can get into before we leave. I'm sure we can party on another nigga's dime again that's trying to impress."

They headed out of the suite and toward the elevator. As they waited, someone called out to them. "I know y'all ain't leaving without telling a nigga bye," Twin Star said.

"You've been pretty occupied, but I was going to send a thank you note for such great hospitality. I had an awesome time," Lexi said, sounding like a professional business woman.

"Yes, Twin Star, you're a wonderful host," Bianca added, remembering some of those etiquette lessons she learned from Mabel.

All he could do was laugh. From the outside they had stone cold, gold digging hoes written all across them, but they gave the aura of not giving a shit one way or another. He had watched several of his boys try to get at them and they gave none of them play. They seemed to be there just to enjoy the night and have fun. He wondered if they were suits like his brother that had decided to hit up Vegas and let their hair down for once. He thought maybe they were on some kind of business conference and smiled at the thought of their uppity coworkers seeing them in their women of the night attire. He was drawn to them both, and even if only for a night, he wanted a little more.

"Thank you, ladies, for gracing me with your company, even though I wasn't able to fully enjoy it." He figured he'd throw the pretty talk right back at them. "I'm not sure how long you ladies are in town, but you only live once, right? Continue the day with me, the rest of the weekend, if possible. It's all on me and away from everyone else, if you choose."

"What exactly does away from everyone else mean?" Lexi asked.

"I have another suite just for me. I let my homies and the hoes stay and party where we just were, but I need my privacy."

"I can feel that. So, where is this private suite?"

"Next floor up."

"It's early, we need sleep."

Twin Star laughed. "You're right, it is early. Let my driver take you to your suite, then later he can take you to the mall to do some shopping and tonight we'll meet up here at my suite."

Lexi looked at Bianca. A free shopping trip and partying on someone sounded good to both of them. They had said they were going to find someone else to party with, but they knew Twin Star was the payout they were looking for. "Are you saying your driver is at our disposal and it's all on you?"

"Everything is on me until this evening. If you don't show up later tonight, then you're welcome for anything I have provided and maybe we'll catch up with each other at another time."

"You straight up. I like that. We're going to get a little rest, and will be at your suite later looking better than any of them five dollar hoes you've ever fucked with." Lexi stepped a little closer to Twin Star, gave him a hug, and kissed him. She pulled Bianca closer to share in the kiss. "See you later, daddy," she said when they finally got on the elevator.

Twin Star was speechless. He wanted them so bad he didn't know what to do. He sure hoped they kept their promise and showed up later. He called his driver and told them to take the girls where ever they needed to go and to bring them back to his private suite at the end of the day. He didn't know what they were into, but he would pay anything to find out.

"I swear, I think you got a dick," Bianca said when they were inside of the limo. She had been around the block a few times, but she enjoyed letting Lexi take the lead. She was used to someone else calling the shots for her and she was comfortable in that position.

"Pussy rule the world. That nigga fine as fuck, though."

"Bitch, you ain't neva lied!" The girls hi-fived each other. "I was high as fuck off that coke. I fucked around a couple of times, but I ain't never felt like that." Bianca was used to getting high to get her job done. Most of the ballers she fucked got high and she always wanted to make them feel comfortable.

"That was my first time. I think I'm still high, but my body telling me I need to rest." Lexi drank and smoked weed from time to time, but that was the extent of her drug use. She saw what drugs did to her parents and never wanted to be like that.

"I feel you. Me too."

They pulled up in front of their hotel and the driver got out and opened their door. He handed Bianca his card. "Call me whenever you're ready."

"Thank you."

The girls went upstairs, showered, and crashed. A few hours later, they woke up and felt rejuvenated. They showered and got dressed in simple jeans, t-shirts, and sandals. Bianca called

Travis, the driver, and within moments he was there. He drove them to the mall and they did a little shopping. When they were done, they told the driver to go ahead and take them to Twin Star's suite. The driver informed them he had to handle some business, but his suite was open for them. He drove them there, and the concierge escorted them to the penthouse suite where he stayed.

"Dayum, bitch! This shit is hella fucking laid!"

"Yea, this some boss shit."

The girls walked around and inspected the entire suite inch by inch. It was beyond their wildest imaginations. They filled the enormous Jacuzzi with water, and both of them got in with two bottles of champagne.

Lexi laid her head back. "This is the fuckin' life." With all the bubbles, she felt like it was right out of the scene from *Scarface*.

"You can say that again. I wonder if this nigga gonna be gone half the night and come creeping in at like five in the morning or some shit."

"It don't even matter. We came here on some solo shit, anyways. If that nigga take too long, we can get fly and head out to do our own thang."

"I wish I had bitches like you in my life back in the day. I was around nothing ass bitches that had nothing ass aspirations. You hold your own, but at the same time you know your worth. You don't let niggas get over on you or play you."

"I'm still new to all this shit. You hold your own, too. Bank Roll always spoke highly of you and never talked against me being around you. Everything happens for a reason, and I believe you were supposed to be in my life."

"Straight up. Now, let's take back these bottles and hit another line."

"Let's do it."

The girls got out of the Jacuzzi and walked into the living room. They ordered room service, mostly appetizers, and had a few more bottles sent up. There was a mound of coke left in one of the rooms, but they didn't want to indulge too much. Lexi liked the high coke gave her. When she was high, she didn't care that she was basically homeless, her money was low, and she didn't know

what the next day held for her. All she cared about was the moment she was in, and at that moment, she felt wonderful.

Twin Star walked in to see them naked on the couch watching *Sparkle*. They were drinking champagne and singing along with the movie.

"Dayum, I didn't expect to walk into such a lovely sight."

"Took you long enough," the snappy Lexi responded with her arms across her chest.

"I had a long day. If I would have known you two were here waiting for me, I would have cut all that short."

"Your driver didn't let you know?"

"He's just working for me while I'm out here. He just does what I say, he don't inform me on certain things."

"Oh, OK," was all Lexi said.

"So, what do you ladies want to do?"

"We're here to chill with you."

Twin Star was distracted by their naked bodies. They seemed so comfortable and spoke with him as if they were fully clothed. Bianca got up and popped another bottle of champagne. Lexi turned on the music and they began to dance for him. Twin Star laid back on the couch and enjoyed the show. The girls danced slowly and provocatively, making him harder by the second. Lexi walked away while Bianca straddled Twin and started kissing him. She gyrated on his lap, and she loved the way his hands felt on her body. She could feel his dick through his jeans and he was definitely packing as she had heard. She was happy the rumors were true. She heard Lexi filling the Jacuzzi again, and then she rejoined them on the couch. They all kissed and fondled each other. When Lexi figured the tub was full she grabbed Twin and Bianca's hand, and led them to it. They undressed Twin, and they all got in the water.

"Damn, you girls gonna turn me out."

Lexi smiled. "It's like you said, you only live once, right? How often can me and my homegirl say we ran into a hot rapper and was able to chill with him solo?"

"Naw, I'm the lucky one tonight."

They continued kissing and Bianca stroked him under water. She wanted to feel him inside of her so bad. The

anticipation of the night had them all on edge. Even Lexi was ready to get the real party started. Twin played with both of their clits. The moaning from them had him going crazy. Lexi grabbed a condom from the side of the Jacuzzi and slid it on Twin. Her plan was to make Bianca his girl, so she motioned for Bianca to get on top of Twin and ride him. When they got into a groove, Lexi stood on the platform of the tub so Twin could taste her pussy. She held her lips open, giving him full access to her clit. Twin had encountered many threesomes, but the one at the moment was different. He was feeling both girls and he wanted it to be more than a one night stand. He put a lashing on Lexi's pussy, licking and sucking as if he would never get the chance to do it again while Bianca bounced on his dick, making him want to cum.

"We need to get out of this water," he finally suggested.

The trio went into the room to the huge bed. Twin put on another condom and Bianca continued to fuck him. Lexi sat on his face, determined to get the orgasm she had been cheated out of from his suggestion. As Bianca rode Twin, she leaned over and began sucking Lexi's perky nipples. Lexi leaned down and rubbed Bianca's clit. When Lexi finally came, she wanted some dick.

"Girl, come get some of this tongue. This nigga the bomb."

The girls switched, and Bianca sat on Twin's face while Lexi sat on his dick after he changed the condom. He filled her insides, and Lexi rode him slowly at first to get used to his length and girth. When she got in a good groove, she leaned back and held onto Twin's feet as she grinded on his dick. Bianca leaned over and began sucking on Lexi's protruding clit as Twin fingered her ass and sucked her pussy.

"Hell yea, bitch, suck that pussy good," Lexi whispered. "That tongue feel good, don't it?"

"Mmmhmm," Bianca moaned.

"Ride that tongue and make me bust on this dick."

Bianca held onto Lexi's thighs as she tasted her sweet pussy and occasionally licked some of Twin's dick. Lexi started gyrating faster as did Bianca. They both began cumming on Twin's face and dick. Lexi got up, and Bianca took off the condom and began sucking Twin's dick as he continued to softly lick her sensitive clit. Lexi joined her girl, and they tag teamed his dick,

making his toes curl. Not able to take his tongue anymore, Bianca finally got off his face and focused on his dick. As they both licked and sucked, he finally exploded with a scream.

"Damn, it's hot. I need something to drink," he said.

popped open another bottle and walked over to the girls. They drank from the bottle until it was empty. Then, Twin brought over a mirror with three lines. "Y'all get on my level. I'm tearing both y'all pussy up 'til we pass out. They all took a line, and Twin bent Bianca over the bed to fuck her from behind. Lexi laid out in front of her so she could eat her pussy. "Yea, suck that sweet ass pussy. Make her cum in your mouth," Twin said as he beat up the pussy. Lexi lifted her legs and put her feet behind her head, giving Bianca all pussy. "Oh shit!" Twin said when he saw that. He fucked Bianca while she ate Lexi's pussy, but he wanted to fuck Lexi in that position. "Go sit on her face so she can eat that pussy," Twin directed. Bianca did as told, and Twin began fucking Lexi. He leaned over and licked Bianca's ass while Lexi licked her clit, and their tongues met often.

They fucked in every position in every way until the sun came up and went down again. It was the next evening when Lexi stood at the window taking in Vegas. She looked back toward the bed at Bianca and Twin. They were fast asleep, and she laid on his chest like she was his woman.

"Yea, that's just the way I want it to be," Lexi whispered. She then went to the bathroom to take a long, hot shower.

CHAPTER 15

It had been a couple of months since the wild weekend with Twin Star and just like Lexi predicted, him and Bianca became somewhat of an item. When he was in town they always kicked it, and she met him in other states occasionally when he did shows. Lexi told him she was married with kids and the weekend was just that, a wild weekend for her memory bank.

Lexi hung out with them sometimes, but nothing sexually happened between them again. She never passed up a free trip so when Twin Star flew Bianca somewhere to kick it with him, Lexi was there in the places she wanted to be. They had been to New York, Chicago, Miami, and Houston. In between that, Lexi used her skills and stripped in San Francisco to keep money coming in. It was the trip to Los Angeles for Lexi's sixteenth birthday where things took a turn in her life.

It was a usual afternoon. While Twin Star handled business, the girls were free to hang out and do what they wanted. They hit up the Beverly Center and burned up the credit card to make sure they looked hot that night for Twin's performance. Since it was Lexi's birthday, they went all out and got her a table and Twin had someone decorate it with balloons, streamers, and he bought her a huge cake with her picture on it. She was in for the surprise of her life and had no idea.

As they were sitting at Roscoe's eating lunch and talking about how wild they knew the night was going to be, they were approached.

"Two gorgeous women like you have got to be taken already."

"We are," Lexi said curtly.

"Figured as much. Are you ladies actresses? Your faces seem familiar."

"Don't think so."

"Well, I do a few movies. Call me if you're ever interested in being on the big screen." He slid his card on the middle of the table and walked away.

"I bet he does do movies," Lexi said as he walked away. The girls giggled and enjoyed their lunch.

When they got back to the room, they got dressed and were ready to party like rock stars.

"Nobody would ever guess your lil' ass just turned sixteen instead of the twenty four you tell 'em," Bianca said.

"Shit, no matter the age, we 'bout to kick it hard."

"You got that right. Damn, when I turned sixteen, all I got was a few blunts and a bottle. I never would have imagined partying in VIP with one of the hottest rappers out there."

"Well, we'll act like it's your birthday, too, and we can both be bad ass sixteen year old bitches partying it up better than grown ass chicks."

"To sixteen," Bianca said as she help up her champagne glass.

Lexi was surprised to see how things were set up for her. She never expected the set up, and she was once again grateful to have a friend like Bianca. They did their usual, partying like the night belonged to them. Lexi was feeling herself as she downed drank after drank. A few hours into the night, Bianca elbowed her.

"Look at that shit right there."

Lexi looked down to the first floor and saw Twin hugged up with some groupie chick as she whispered in his ear. "Bitch, who he paying? Fuck that nothing ass hoe."

"I can't believe he gonna holla at her knowing I'm here. It's your fucking birthday."

Lexi shook her head. "Grab this damn drank and shake that shit off. Niggas come a dime a dozen, remember that."

"You right, girl."

Bianca pretended to be unfazed, but she eyed Twin and the girl until they disappeared down a hall. He emerged about twenty minutes later zipping his zipper. She felt played, but she shook it off.

A couple of days had passed, and Twin Star and Bianca were boo'd up. That left Lexi alone and she didn't know what to do. She pulled out the guy's card from a few days ago and looked at it. *All Night Productions. Harold Black, CEO.* She laughed to herself because she had a couple All Night Productions movies. She was bored with life as it was, so she decided to give him a call.

"Harold Black speaking," he answered.

"Hey, this Lexi, the chocolate chick from the other day you gave your card to at Roscoe's."

"Hey, you. I didn't think I would hear from you."

"Got a lil' bored. So, what's All Night Productions?" She laid back on the couch and took a sip of champagne, ready to hear whatever kind of line Harold was about to feed her.

"We do adult films. Very tasteful."

"Hmm, I'm not really interested in tasteful. I like gutta shit."

Harold's dick jumped at her straight to the point vibe. "Is that right?"

Lexi had taken two lines and was feeling herself. Twin Star supplied unlimited coke and although she tried to limit herself, she enjoyed the high and indulged when she wanted. "How about you send a car to pick me up and bring me to your studio, and I can show you?"

"That's what I like to hear." Harold had already started the text to his driver, he just needed the location.

Lexi gave him her info and within an hour, she was at his studio. It was a big warehouse and although she wasn't sure what a porn studio should look like, she didn't complain. Lexi hadn't paid Harold much attention earlier, but on second look he was fine. He was tall and light skinned with shoulder length dreads. He didn't have that creepy porno look, he looked like a regular nigga. He took Lexi into his office to talk a little bit, and she told him she was interested in at least doing a test run. She had never thought of doing porn before, but it was the exciting change she felt she

needed at that time. Looking at those sexy eyes, it didn't take much convincing for Harold. He led her to the test room and paired her with one of his best men.

Xtreme was the best of the best, and he was good at breaking in newbies. He could tell if a girl was just talking shit to step outside of the box or if they were ready for the business. Lexi wasted no time. She walked up to him, dropped to her knees, and began sucking his dick. Xtreme was longer and thicker than Twin Star, but she handled him like a pro. She spat on his dick and used her hands as she almost brought him to the brink of cumming.

"Whoa, lil' chocolate, you vicious."

He laid her back on the bed, lifted her skirt, and began licking her pussy. She held his head as she talked shit to him. After she came, he put on a condom and worked himself inside of her. The way she sucked his dick he knew someone had to be banging her out, but she was tight. Lexi hadn't fucked since the wild night with Twin Star and Bianca. She was a very sexual person, but random fucking had never been her thing. She was horny and fucking the sexy porn star was just what she needed.

She played with her clit as he eased himself all the way inside of her. He pushed her legs back as far as he could and began deep stroking her. Lexi closed her eyes for a moment to get a grip on the situation. She adjusted to Xtreme's dick, and then began throwing it on him. Her pussy was good and juicy, making squishy sounds as he pounded her. He pulled out and smacked her thigh.

"Turn over."

Lexi got on her hands and knees, and opened her legs for Xtreme to enter her from the back. Her toes curled as he hit that spot repeatedly. She tried to calm herself and heard Bank Roll's voice. 'Don't let that nigga turn you out by hitting that G spot over and over. Own ya shit and turn that nigga out, baby girl.' Lexi got a hold of herself and allowed her orgasms to flow freely on Xtreme's dick. She knew she came at least three times, and she kept on going.

"Lay down and let me ride that dick," she said to him.

Xtreme laid on the bed and Lexi got on top of him backwards. She got on her feet and held onto his legs for balance. She bounced on his dick like she was riding a thoroughbred horse.

Xtreme held onto her hips and enjoyed the ride as her ass slapped against his body.

"Shit, you gonna make me cum," he said through pants.

Lexi bounced a little more, and then she jumped off of him, took the condom off, and sucked his dick. When he came, she let him skeet all over her face and tits. After he caught his breath, he looked at Harold.

"Yea, she good to go."

Harold had a wide smile across his face. "Let's talk business."

Lexi followed him to his office and they got everything together. She whipped out the fake ID she had held onto proudly for a while. She signed the paperwork and became was the new All Night Productions girl. She decided to keep her real name. No one could be as savage as Lexi when it came to freaking.

Things went quick. Only two weeks had gone by and she had already been in four movies. She made a decent amount of money stripping, but it went to another level with the movies. She had instantly become a high commodity, and everybody wanted to shoot a scene with her. Lexi couldn't front, she loved busting nuts, but busting nuts for paychecks did something totally different for her. Porn was her calling, at least for that moment.

CHAPTER 16

"I can't believe your ass doing porn."

"I never would have imagined that shit, but it pays good and a bitch stay fucking."

"Shit, thinking of it I'm sure it's better than hoeing. Bank Roll never set me up with raggedy niggas, but with porn you get yours, too."

"Not always. I know a lot of bitches that get pounded out for a lil' bit of money. You see it's only a few bitches that be featured in a lot of movies. A lot of them hoes be just that, some dumb ass hoes that got an E pill and a few bucks to fuck on camera."

"That nigga Xtreme got a big ass dick."

"That shit feel so good. It's hard not to get sprung on that shit. All them bitches be jocking him 'cause you really will thinking he making love to you. You know I'm not the bitch to jock a nigga or be on a nigga that got hella bitches on him. We have a good working relationship."

"What's up with that Marlon Mann nigga?"

"Girl, he puts it down, too. He love eating pussy, and you know when a bitch high it take a while to nut. He will eat that pussy forever, fuck, and then eat it again."

"That bitch Cherry Bomb is hella fine."

"She thick as fuck. She got some good ass pussy. That shit get hella wet and her soft moans sound good. Me and her hooked up a couple times outside of shooting."

Leila Jefferson

Lexi thought back to the first time they hung out. Cherry picked her up and they went out to dinner. During that time, Cherry damn near told Lexi her entire life story. Her life of sex began when she was eleven, just like Lexi. Her brother and three younger sisters lived in a small, two bedroom apartment. There was a bunk bed and a baby bed. Paul, Cherry's brother, slept on the couch until the girls pissed it out so bad he couldn't stand it. Then, he slept on the floor, but the roaches and mice bit him while he tried to sleep. Finally, he asked Cherry if he could sleep in the top bunk with her. Having no problem sleeping with her older brother like they did when they were younger, Cherry said yes.

A few days had passed and although Cherry hadn't found herself thinking about boys, at fourteen, Paul was definitely thinking about girls but he was broke with raggedy, handed down clothes so no one thought about giving him any conversation. He hadn't grown into his looks and was awkward. Cherry, on the verge of blossoming into a young woman, began to have curves and a lil' butt that stuck out with perky titties. One night, the brother and sister were in bed sleep, and Cherry felt something poking her back. She turned around to face Paul and asked him was he OK. Embarrassed, he told her to go to sleep. He knew he was wrong, but Cherry was finer than any girl he had ever seen, even if she was his sister. Her smooth, cocoa skin seemed to glow and even though her hair wasn't maintained, it was long and pretty. She had long legs and plump titties he always thought about as he laid next to her. There were nights he slightly grinded against her until he came, and although Cherry was awake most nights, she laid stiff as a board while her brother handled his business.

After a few nights, Cherry got bold and reached behind her to grab her brother's hardness. He didn't stop her, he continued to grind as she moved her hand up and down his shaft. She liked the way it felt and when he came, he whispered, "I love you, my Cherry Bomb. No nigga will ever love you the way I do."

"I love you, too," she whispered.

As time went on, they progressed from her jacking him off to him sucking her swollen nipples and rubbing on her clit. Both of them curious and wanting more, he finally penetrated her, professing his love in her ear while she did the same. Having a

130

mother who only cared about her next high and her next trick, they found something special in each other as they cared for their little sisters and waited for nightfall to hit so they could love each other until they passed out.

Things took a drastic turn about a year later when their mother called herself having a boyfriend. Cherry and Paul could see the way he looked at her, and they planned to run away so they could be together forever. Before that happened, Mitch made his way in the room, pushed Paul to the side, and told him it was his turn to get some of that young, hot pussy. He knew Cherry and Paul had been fucking because he often stood outside the door and listened to them as they tried to be quiet.

Paul jumped up, determined not to let Mitch have any of his Cherry Bomb. He rushed him, and Mitch easily pushed him off and flung him out of the way. With Paul unconscious, Mitch grabbed Cherry, pried her legs open, and forced himself inside of her, pumping furiously until he came.

Cherry cried while she sat next to Paul and tried to wake him. When he finally came to, he vowed to kill Mitch. With his mother passed out, he stormed in the room with a knife. Mitch, overpowering Paul, wrestled the knife from him and killed him. He raped Cherry every night after that until she ran away.

Lexi felt so bad. She could feel that even though he was her brother, Cherry loved Paul just as much as she loved Bank Roll. They both had forbidden loves, and their loves were ripped away from their lives so suddenly. From that day, they were close friends.

"Hello, bitch! Damn, did you get lost?" Bianca asked.

"Just had a few thoughts. Anyways, what's been good with you and Twin?"

"It's whatever. He been working a lot, on the grind trying to come up. He take care of me and in turn, I can take care of my family. I feel bad sometimes 'cause I don't really fuck with them, but my life too wild. I'm glad my sister realized that and raise my babies like her own."

"She good peoples. I'm glad you got someone like her in your corner. I know you want to be there for your kids, but at least she's the next best thing."

"I feel so guilty sometimes, Lex. I was always told my maternal instincts would kick in, but I don't think they did. I ain't even told Twin I have kids. How fucked up is that?"

"You trying to be with this nigga?"

"I don't know, Lex, I'm feeling him."

"The question is, is he feeling you? I seen how you was hawking that nigga on my birthday. Niggas like him come a dime a dozen. How you know he ain't flying out other bitches when you ain't around? Twin a cool ass nigga, but at the end of the day he a nigga. It's his job to make you feel like you the only one. How many threesomes have you freaked with him? Were they random bitches or bitches he called up to come hang with you? I hella loved Bank Roll with everything I had and you kept me in check. Now, I'm here to do the same for you."

Bianca looked like she was thinking about everything Lexi just said. She had definitely had her share of threesomes with Twin. In every city, not matter how small, he always had someone to call. It seemed like the only time they spent alone was when Lexi was on a trip with them. Twin knew the married with kids story was straight bullshit and he wanted her again. No matter how high he got her and how many bottles they downed, Lexi didn't bite. He kept Bianca around in hopes of getting at Lexi just once more, and both girls got quite a bit of trinkets as their reminder of their run with Twin Star.

Bianca sighed. "He gives me the some sort of solidity. We have no titles, but I feel like I can call him my dude."

"He's done a gang of interviews. Has he ever mentioned you? Has he ever had you walk the red carpet with him and take pics? Come on, B, you know your worth. I ain't got to the point where I want to be boo'd up and I can tell that's something you want, but you don't want it with him."

"I know, I know. It's a great fantasy, though. Have the baller boyfriend and living in the humongous house with unlimited funds."

"You can have that, but it comes with consequences. Are you ready for that? Can you tolerate him being gone for days, weeks, and you don't talk to him? I know you got it in you, but not if you in love, and you are."

"I don't know what happened," Bianca confessed.

"You been saying you lonely and you wanna be boo'd up. I shouldn't have put you on Twin knowing that. If you want to ride this out, then I got your back."

"I'm just going to play it by ear. I mean, we just chillin', we having fun."

"If it's just chilling and fun, then check ya feelings at the door. Don't fool yourself and get hurt."

"Shit, I always love it when I get a good dose of you. He gone for a few weeks, anyways. I need the break to get my head out the clouds."

"What you gonna do while he gone?"

"Moving. I stacked enough money from him to get a lil' house out in Stockton. Imma move my sister and momma there, and, of course, the kids."

"Go 'head, bitch. That's all good. Bank Roll would be proud of a boss move like that. Just make sure you keep up them payments."

Bianca laughed. "I got you."

"That's some cool shit for the kids. I remember going to my aunt's house, not apartment, and just chilling. It's a freeing thing to a kid to be able to go in the back yard and enjoy life. Why is it houses seem more stable than apartments?" Lexi asked, thinking back to all the ghetto places she had lived in her younger days.

"'Cause they are. I feel so proud. We ain't never lived in a house. Not my momma, my sister, none of us."

"Gotta break the cycle and start something better sooner or later."

"Yea."

"Well, when you finish moving, you need to come out here and visit me. It's about time for us to get together and wild out. I miss you, hoe."

"I miss you, too, Ms. Porn Star."

"Yea, right."

"I bought one of your movies the other day. Bitch, you be putting it down."

"'Cause I'm a Savage. When I do something, I go hard."

"So, is this what you doing now?"

"For now. I'm not trying to make a lifelong commitment. It's fun and I get fucked hella good with no strings attached. Muthafuckas will be looking at my ass for years to come and jack off. Pussy rule the muthafuckin' world."

"You got that right."

"Girl, get you enough money to pay off that house before you stop fucking with Twin. And, make sure you get a hot ass car."

"You know I already flipped a car. Got a Benz SLK, it's hot."

"Ahh shit. I can't wait to ride in it."

"My momma just told me dinner ready. Can you believe that? We all having dinner together."

"Keep those family ties close. I envy you."

"I'm trying. I want to do things different, so these next few weeks I'm going to try."

"That's all you can do. Love you."

"Love you, too, girl. Talk to you soon."

Lexi hung up and smiled for her friend. Being around her aunt and cousins, she always wanted to sit with her sister and parents, and have dinner. She wanted them to help her with homework and encourage her to be better. Instead, she basically got sold for an unlimited high. Bank Roll had been great to her, but it still wasn't an ideal situation.

Lexi leaned back on the leather couch. She knew how Bianca felt because living the lavish life had her hooked. She had started fucking with Harold and she lived in his humongous home. It looked like something straight off of *MTV Cribs*. The house was so big, a few families could live there and they would never bump into each other. Harold hosted many parties and even filmed there from time to time. It was always in Lexi's nature to find the one running it and conquer them. Harold was a piece of cake.

She knew the best way to have a man lusting after her was to ignore him. When she 'accidently' confessed to Harold she was

134

living motel to motel, he told her he had plenty of rooms at his house and she was more than welcomed to one until she got herself together. At first, they rarely saw each other. He was busy and she was always on set. She made sure she wasn't home when he was, and she wasn't at the set when she knew he was going to be there. That worked well for the first few weeks. They were strangers living in the same house.

When Harold extended the offer, he thought she would be like the rest of the girls who threw themselves at him the first night. All of the girls that he offered a room to before stalked him. They walked around naked and crawled in his bed in the middle of the night. In his lifetime of porn, he had gotten more pussy than he could have ever imagined.

He loved women. Always had. He could remember giving his babysitter big hugs and lying down with her to take naps to feel her soft titties. He always held onto ladies' legs and rubbed them while they paid him no mind to a little boy being manish.

When he got a little older, around nine, his babysitter then was twelve. Nikki Towns was the hot ass around the neighborhood and loved to babysit to have boys over since her parents were so strict. Nikki caught Harold peeking at her while she was in the shower after sexing some guy, and she let him come in and feel her titties and even her hot box. When she couldn't find someone to come over and fuck her, she let Harold suck her titties and rub her clit until she came.

When he was eleven, he had sex for the first time. Nikki had moved away and Harold was fiending to feel a girl again. He got his wish with the girl that, ironically, moved into Nikki's old house. She was fourteen, and she always had a hot box that needed to be hosed often. Harold was tall for his age. Being around Nikki, he learned how not to be an overeager boy in the presence of a pretty girl. Nikki had played with his dick and even sucked it a few times. She told him he had a big dick for his age and young girls wouldn't be able to handle it. She told him she was going to give him his first feel of pussy when she thought he was ready, but she moved before it happened.

Carmen was walking down the street when Harold first saw her. After that day, they said hello and bye, and exchanged smiles.

It wasn't until about a month later until they actually had a conversation. Harold saw Carmen sitting on the porch crying. He approached her and asked what was wrong. She told him about catching her boyfriend cheating with her friend. Harold sat there and let her cry on his shoulder. Before he knew it, she was kissing him, and then she asked if he wanted to go inside of her house. He felt it was the moment he had been waiting for, but he shrugged his shoulders and said he should be getting home. After she all but begged, he finally followed behind her inside of her house.

He wasn't fully aware of rebound sex so as he coolly sat there on her couch while she got him a glass of Kool-Aid, she returned in nothing but her bra and panties. She pounced on him, wanting to get back at her boyfriend and fuck someone else. As she kissed Harold's body he sat almost motionless, not wanting to do anything to mess up. He let her take control, and she did it so well. He came quick the first time, but he played with her pussy and sucked her titties as he had done with Nikki so many times. Seconds later his dick was hard again, and he gave her a run for her money putting her in various positions, savoring the warm gushy.

When she found out he was just eleven she felt embarrassed, but he fucked her so good he was her little secret for a few years. He wasn't really a secret, she had told a few of her girlfriends about his skills, and soon, many of the teenage girls were after him to hit their spot and make them cum over and over. By the time he was in high school, his reputation had proceeded him and he was more popular than he could have imagined. He was a player, a ladies' man, and the girls had no problem with waiting in line to be next.

He knew he was interested in film, and porn was the last thing on his mind until senior year. There was a party going on and his skillful smooth talk had two girls giving a show in the middle of the room. He softly talked to them, guiding them into giving the audience the best show they had ever witnessed. It was the nonchalant comment of, 'Damn, that nigga need to direct porns and shit,' that got him started in a lucrative business that paid him well.

Harold wanted Lexi the first time he saw her. He usually didn't go for the chocolate girls, but there was something about those sexy ass eyes and that exotic look that pulled him in. On top of that, she was so professional. He thought she wasn't fucking with him because she had a boyfriend, but he hadn't known of her talking to anyone and neither had anyone else they worked with. He left her little gifts saying they were for her great performances, but they both knew that wasn't the case.

Lexi finally made her move one night. Cherry Bomb was on the phone with her and during casual conversation, Cherry mentioned Harold had just left the studio and said he was going home to crash because he had had a long few days. Lexi was glad she had just gotten out of the shower, so all she needed to do was put on something that smelled good. She got off the phone and went in her room to spray on Chanel No. 5.

"Can't go wrong with this," she whispered.

Being that he could walk in the house and they not run into each other, she decided to go against the coy approach and put it out there. She was at the bottom of the stairwell in her birthday suit when Harold walked through the door. He was looking down at his phone, not paying attention to his surroundings. He smelled her first. When he looked up and saw Lexi standing there butt naked, he didn't say a word. He tossed his phone on the small table near the door and grabbed Lexi into a kiss. He wasn't going to fuck off the opportunity with small talk and get some bullshit about she didn't expect him to be home and give apologies before rushing upstairs. He picked her up and carried her to the couch. Without a word, he spread her legs and finally did what he had been dying to do since he laid eyes on her. He ate her pussy with no mercy. Lexi moaned and crawled up the couch. She laughed inside thinking about shooting a scene on that exact couch about two weeks prior. She pulled Harold up, licked her juices off his lips, and tore off his clothes. She dropped down and sucked the life out of his dick as he held on for the ride. Not wanting him to cum, she stood up and placed one leg on the couch while one remained on the floor. Harold positioned himself behind her, bent her over, and fucked her dry. They showered together, fucked again, and after that night, Lexi was Harold's girl.

CHAPTER 17

Lexi was in the Bay Area visiting Bianca. She hadn't seen her in a while so she decided to make an appearance. Twin performed at a club in San Francisco and the girls were there having their usual ball of a time. As Lexi scanned the crowd, she saw a face she hadn't seen in years. She blinked hard just to make sure she wasn't seeing things, and then she pushed her way through the crowd. Bianca, not knowing what was going on, followed her in case she needed to have her back.

Lexi, where you going?" she asked, trying to keep up with her.

Lexi was quiet, she was on a mission. She rudely bumped past partygoers, ignoring their disgusted sighs and slew of cuss words. Finally, she was face to face with her. "Lexi?" she questioned, already knowing the answer.

"Sin! I haven't seen you in so long. What's been up? How are you? What are you doing here?" She didn't expect answers, but the questions flew out of her mouth one after another. She grabbed her sister and hugged her. "Let's go outside and talk."

"Hey, girl!" Bianca said when she finally saw that Lexi was trying to catch up to Yesina.

"Bianca, it's been years. Y'all looking good."

"So are you." Lexi actually meant it when she said it. There weren't bruises and Yesina was drop dead gorgeous in a red mini dress that hugged her curvy body.

They walked outside and the sisters talked. Lexi wondered why Yesina never came to look for her when she left, but she knew what it was. Yesina wondered why Lexi chose to leave in the middle to the night, but she had a good idea Todd had something to do with it although she never said anything. They talked a mile a minute, trying to fill each other on everything when a guy walked up to them.

"Baby, I was looking all over for you." He put his arm around Yesina's waist and kissed her cheek.

"I'm sorry, looked who I bumped into."

"Sexi Lexi," he said as he looked at her with lust in his eyes.

Lexi raised her brows. "Someone likes porn, huh?"

"I've caught a couple in my lifetime."

Lexi just looked at him. "So, Sin, where you at now?"

"San Leandro. You should come over tomorrow and hang out."

"I can do that."

"Damn, we got a lot of catching up."

"Well, come to VIP with us and chill for the rest of the night."

"Oh, hell yea, that's what's up," Todd responded.

The next day, Lexi got up as early as she could and headed to her sister's. Her apartment wasn't horrible, but Lexi expected more. Todd wasn't home and that made Lexi happy. She wanted some alone time to get the 411.

"So, what's been up?"

"Everything. I've gone through the ups and downs with Todd hard, but I love him. When I found out I was having twins I almost shitted on myself. I want to do better for them, though. I'm thinking of going to school."

"That's great."

"So, what's good with you?"

"I'm just living life."

"How the hell did you get into porn?"

"Chance meeting. Me and Bianca were in LA chilling and Harold walked up to us and dropped off his card. Bianca left to chill with Twin, so I called the nigga up and the rest is history."

"How you feel fucking in front of cameras?"

"Don't make me none. The money good and I love the party life."

"I don't even party that much. Last night was the first time I was out in a while. I stopped by Auntie Lizzie's 'bout a year or so ago. No one was there but her and that was a good thing. We chatted a lil' bit."

"She's always been good peoples. I haven't seen her since I left her house that night."

"Why didn't you stay to finish school and stuff?"

Lexi shook her head. "Just wasn't the life for me. Auntie Lizzie was hardly home 'cause she worked so much, so me and Christy freak ass got away with a lot, but I was tired of it."

"Christy a freak?"

"You have no idea. She fucked a gang of dicks the little while I was there, no telling how many more she fucked."

"Damn, that's crazy."

They talked a little more, and then Todd walked in with a few of his friends. Lexi could tell he brought them over to stare in her face. She wasn't ashamed of her job, but she didn't like how he seemed to be overly excited. Yesina spoke to his friends, and then Todd introduced them to Lexi with a wide grin on his face.

"Damn, I've seen all your movies," one of them said.

"You need to let me wear that ass out," another said.

Lexi laughed while Yesina got visibly upset. "Leave her alone."

"It's good, sis." Lexi shook her head as she looked them all up and down. "Trust, y'all can't afford me, and you damn sure can't handle me."

"You don't know what I can afford."

Lexi smirked. "You right, but again, you can't afford me." Lexi looked at her sister. "Girl, I got a few runs I need to make, but I'll be back before I head back home."

"You better come back."

Lexi jumped in the car and rode around. She loved LA, the partying, the nightlife, the shopping, but there was no place like home. Bianca offered her to stay at her place, but she didn't want to impose on their newfound family life. Instead, she got a room at

the Motel 6 on Hegenburger until she figured out what she was going to do. She had plenty of money to stay somewhere else, but she loved being in the heart of the hood.

She finally stopped at Bank Roll's grave. She hadn't visited him in a while and needed to talk. She pulled up to the cemetery and parked the clean ass BMW she had borrowed from Bianca. She grabbed the bag that contained the pint of Hennessy to go with her coke. She slowly walked toward his tombstone and sat down next to it. She cleared the dead flowers and placed the fresh ones she bought. She cracked open her bottle and took a swig.

"Damn, daddy, I miss you. I know you know I been living a wild life, but that's who I am, right?" She pulled out a compact, made two lines, and then sniffed them. "I didn't know I would hurt so bad not having you. This powder the magic elixir, I don't feel so much pain." She leaned against his tombstone and let her tears fall. "Then, this nigga wanna go and ask me to marry him. I ain't the marrying type, daddy. Sex is our business, we have no business trying to do normal people shit."

That was really the reason Lexi popped up in the Bay Area. Her and Harold had gone to dinner. Like one of those cheesy romance movies, she went to the bathroom and when she returned, there was a huge diamond ring in her champagne glass. Her eyes were wide and her mouth was dropped, but she had no idea what to do. She had never told Harold her real age, she wasn't ready for that kind of commitment, and she felt bad because she was actually feeling him. She started feeling like she had betrayed Bank Roll. She wanted to be strong like her aunt and never love another, but she couldn't deny that she felt something for the man sitting in front of her proposing marriage.

They spent many nights away from each other, but spent many more together. They had gone on a few vacations and there were never any arguments about who was fucking whom. They had a mutual understanding and a mutual respect, and the proposal would change it all. Not knowing what else to do, she slipped away while Harold was doing business and left him a card stating she would talk to him soon.

"Baby girl, you need to slow down. I know you a hustla, but you gotta do shit the right way. I was looking forward to seeing

you walk across the stage. Just because I'm not there in the physical don't mean I'm wasn't going to be there for you." She heard Bank Roll's voice so clearly. She wiped her eyes with her sleeve and looked around.

"Look at my little Lexi. You're a beautiful woman, but what did I tell you? Drugs fuck your worth off. Stop putting that shit up ya nose. Your sister is better now, and you need to get better, too. Get it together and listen to the right instincts to get you through life." That time, it was her daddy that she heard loud and clear.

She looked down at the rest of the powder she had. "Where the fuck did Harold get this shit?" she asked herself.

She sighed. They both were right. She knew she could get her GED, and maybe she could go to Laney and take a few courses until she figured her life out. Drugs had her walking around in a haze. She fucked, sucked, got paid, and lived lavish. She was a shell, not having any real emotions or feelings. She wasn't sure what she wanted to do, but she had to do something.

She wiped her tears and sat there for another hour talking to Bank Roll and her daddy, and even her mother. There were so many things in her life she needed to re-evaluate and she didn't know where to start. She figured she'd let the high wear off and give her life a real thought. While she waited on that, she went to Chili's for a couple of margaritas, and some kind of food to soak up some of the Hennessy and drugs. She tried to force a few chips down her throat, but all she cared about was a top shelf margarita. Once the drink was placed in front of her and she took a big sip, she sat back and exhaled as she looked at the ring.

"Well, well, well, Ms. Savage in the flesh."

Lexi whipped her head around to see Ms. Hope standing there looking sexy as ever. She had on a midnight blue dress with strappy heeled sandals and her hair was up in a bun with a few curled strands framing her face. There was a time when Lexi's heart raced fast at just the sight of the older, very experienced woman. She had been a million miles of places since then, though, so she gave her a once over and picked up her drink.

Ms. Hope sat in the chair across from her. When the waiter returned, he asked if she would be joining and if he could get her

anything. "Yes, I'll have what she's sipping on." She leaned back casually in the seat as if she had been invited. "My little Lexi is a woman now. Well, you always were a woman, but you've grown into it." Lexi remained motionless as she looked at her uninvited guest. "I see you're not amused," she said to break the awkward silence. "Look, I'll go ahead and cut to the chase. Do you believe in destiny, in things happening just the way they are supposed to?"

"Depends," Lexi answered with a shrug, finally breaking her silence.

Ms. Hope was still fine. She had her hair pulled back in a bun and her shape was on point. The low cut top showcased her cleavage while the short skirt make her legs seem a mile long. She was still a class act, but Lexi wanted Ms. Hope out of her face.

The waiter came back with her margarita. When he left, Ms. Hope continued. "About a year ago I was out with some of my friends and I met a guy. He's a regular guy, different from anyone I've ever dated, but he's so sweet and adores me. He asked me to marry him last night and I ran out on him. My life is wild and free, but he offers that normalcy I've been craving. I came here today to weigh the pros and cons of life, and I just told myself if I could find someone to take over my business, I'd marry him and leave."

Lexi almost wanted to confide that she was in almost the same situation. Almost. It did amaze her that they both had been given marriage proposals and they both ran away. With Lexi, she knew Harold could definitely keep up and there would be no normalcy or her having to change anything about her lifestyle. Finally, she said, "What does all this have to do with me?"

"I know things didn't end on the best terms and I'm sorry. If it means anything, I liked you more than the rest," Ms. Hope offered with a seductive smile.

Lexi rolled her eyes. "It doesn't, so get on with it."

"You're a smart girl. I have a business and I know you would be perfect to take over for me."

"How do you know that?" Lexi asked with a raised brow.

"Because, Sexi Lexi Savage, I know you are about *your* business."

Lexi smirked at Ms. Hope addressing her by her porn name. Never one to put emotions over money, she put her elbows

on the table and rested her chin on her hands. "No one knows all my business, Ms. Hope. Keep talking."

"Last time I checked, you were supposed to be eighteen to be in movies, at least that's what the disclaimers say. If my calculations are right, you probably just turned seventeen."

"Well, for anyone that checks, I am at least eighteen." Ms. Hope smiled. "So, what kind of business is this?"

"It's a call girl business, well, call boy. Just like men pay top dollar for a pretty young thang they can fuck, women pay just as much for a young stallion to blow their back out. I have a nice list of customers that consists of doctors, lawyers, business women, singers. And, I have an equally nice stable of young men."

"Why not girls?"

"Too messy, complain, always have issues. You know the saying with boys, young, dumb, and full of cum. They get to fuck top notch bitches and get paid, plus, whatever extras they get from the women. I'm willing to put a goldmine in your lap, all you have to do is say yes."

"What's in it for you?" Lexi knew nothing in life was free.

Ms. Hope raised her hands. "This time, absolutely nothing. Like I first stated, I'm in love and I want to leave this life behind. I've built a reputable business and I didn't want to freeze it, but I didn't want to leave it in the hands of someone not capable. How about this, just come by and take a look at things." She slid a card across the table to Lexi.

"I'll think about it."

"Don't think too long." Ms. Hope finished her drink and then got up to leave.

Lexi sat there for a minute, mindlessly eating a few chips. She knew she would take Ms. Hope up on her offer. If she knew nothing else, she knew sex was an unlimited industry. There were many people that damned sinners to hell, but there were three times as many that accepted their damnation and were all about sex, drugs, and rock and roll. Lexi grabbed her purse to pay the bill and saw that Ms. Hope had left a hundred dollar bill on the table. "Thanks, boo," she said to herself before she left.

She went to her room and knew the next day was the beginning of a new day. She knew Harold wouldn't give her any

slack about leaving. She had filmed more than enough scenes to keep her legacy going for a while.

CHAPTER 18

After Lexi went to Ms. Hope's home and checked out her operation, she was impressed. She knew some things would change, but there were a lot of things she liked. She had seven men that were between the ages of eighteen and twenty four. A couple of the faces Lexi remembered from school, one of them being Rico, the fine brotha that was fucking some dude that was eating Ms. Hope's pussy that night. There were twenty seven women, most of them wanted to be serviced maybe once a month. As things stood, there was never a scheduling conflict. She wasn't running a sleazy nickel and dime set up. She had a couple of standing rooms at the Marriot in a couple of cities. One of her clients was a regional manager and set that up for her. The room fee was included in the booking fee, which was fifteen hundred. Six hundred went to Ms. Hope and the rest to the chosen man. Easy money. She did a background check on the women and the men got tested every six months. They were all chiseled and fine. Lexi met them the next time she entered Ms. Hope's lavish home, a different home than she had visited in high school.

After Lexi was brought up to speed with the entire operation, she thought of the few things she wanted to change. First, she wanted an office to make things feel more official. She didn't want them at her home for meetings or anything else. She wanted a more professional feel to the business, and she knew exactly where she would start.

It took her two months, but with Bianca's help she was ready to go. She had named the business Fantasies, and she had a plush office in a high rise in the financial district of San Francisco. While getting ready for the transition, she found out one of the clients was a photographer and had her take pictures of all the men. She had each of them submit three videos, and before she officially became their boss she had all of them fuck the shit out of her. She knew Ms. Hope knew how to pick them, but she needed to try the product for herself so she could speak highly of what she had to offer.

She had made plenty of connections in LA and Vegas, and knew many people visited the Bay Area for many reasons. Dick would make a woman do anything, and the dick she offered would make a woman kill her own kids for another hit. She wished she could have brought Xtreme to the team, but she didn't want to burn any bridges with that move. Although Ms. Hope didn't want to deal with women, Lexi knew she had to have a couple on her team. She knew too many big spenders that she could make easy money from with having a few top notches on the team. She hired Bianca on as her assistant to allow her steady income since she didn't mess with Twin Star anymore. She wasn't hurt for money, but Lexi wanted someone on the team she trusted.

Their first official meeting was held in the conference room across from the office. There were erotic paintings on the walls, and the room was decorated in gold and black with accents of red. All the guys were present along with Cherry Bomb, Unique, and Tasty.

"OK, everyone, I wanted everyone to officially meet and get a few things together. First off, this sexy little honey dip right here is my right hand, Bianca. You guys don't know her, but we go way back. Respect her like you respect me."

"Hey, I seen you in some flicks," Hung said to Cherry Bomb. Hung got his name because he was hung like a horse and knew how to work his dick, tongue, and fingers. He could have any woman speaking in tongues, no matter how seasoned she was. He made love like he was really in love, and women paid top dollar for what he offered. Lexi found out that even though she thought she was a G, there were a lot of dicks and a lot of niggas

with skills she wasn't prepared for. He hit spots she didn't even know she had while he looked deep in her eyes and sucked the life out of her tongue.

"Yea, that's me," Cherry said with a smile after she blew a kiss.

"First rule, no fucking each other. I don't need the drama that comes from a situation like that." Lexi saw the bad situation that could have happened and deaded that before it could start.

Hung gave a look of defeat. He had seen Cherry in action plenty of times and always talked about what he would do to her if he ever met her. *Maybe in another lifetime*, he thought.

Unique and Tasty were dancers at a club in LA where Lexi made guest appearances. They always told her they wanted to do movies and when Lexi hooked it up for them to audition, they got cold feet. They had turned plenty of tricks, but being in front of a camera for any and everybody to see was a little more than they had bargained for. Lexi knew they would be perfect for what she wanted to do. Wanting a change of scenario, the girls were ready to pack up and check out Bay Area living.

After introductions, they went around the table and shared a little about themselves, how they got in the current situation, and what they wanted out of it. They wanted to help families, support kids, find a better life, and even fund school. No matter the goal, they all shared one common factor, they loved sex and money.

When a few months had passed and Harold hadn't heard from Lexi, he decided to call. Clubs were calling and requesting her for performances, but deep inside he missed her. With most women it was just about a fuck, but he felt something different with her. He knew she had to have felt it, too, and even though she said she needed a little time he needed to know what was up. Getting her voicemail, he left a message for her to call.

He had to be real with himself, he was in love. He had fucked a few bitches after Lexi left, but he missed her. He missed the way she felt snuggled next to him. He missed the way she called him daddy and massaged him after a long day. He missed hearing her laugh at his silly jokes. He missed talking to her. He had opened up to her and shared a lot of his past. He knew they

were meant to be, but he wasn't going to push her. If they were going to be together, it had to be her decision.

Lexi was on a mission. She played phone tag with Harold for months because she knew his schedule and knew there were certain times he wouldn't answer his phone. Getting the business organized to her standards gave her potential for more income. After she secured fifteen more clients, ten being men, she went to Atlanta, New York, and Florida to check out a few places and hit up a few people she had met on her porn ride. When she was out of town, Bianca was in charge of everything and kept business running smoothly. Lexi felt like a boss pimp, and she felt like she was on top of the world. She popped bottles in VIP and made it rain like a pro. When recruiting was done she went back home with three men, Freak, Scorpio, and Dope, and she had another woman, Sassy.

Always thinking ahead of the game, Lexi had a couple of rooms ready for them. She gave them a month to get their money together and make their own way. If they were true hustlers, they wouldn't need that full month to be on her dime. After she got them situated and on the roster, she had to make another trip.

Two months had gone by since Harold first called her. She didn't need to be caught up with him and his emotions while she got her shit together, so she decided to deal with him when it was convenient for her. That was one thing she liked about him, he gave her space. When they lived together, either of them could go days without seeing each other and it was all good. No one nagged the other with never ending questions.

She missed Harold. They were alike in so many ways. When she was alone at night, she found herself thinking of him and wondering if they could really make it work. She asked herself numerous times if she loved him, but at the end of the day she was still convinced it was a four letter word that didn't mean shit to anyone. Love wasn't for niggas from the ghetto who built an empire from sex.

She was feeling him, but what did that mean? In their world, Prince Charming didn't ride up on white horses and carry Snow White or Sleeping Beauty away in the sunset for a life of

love and happiness. They both came from years of pimping, hoeing, sluts, niggas, gold diggers, and dogs. It was what it was, and Lexi accepted that.

CHAPTER 19

Lexi pulled up to the beautiful place she once called home and parked in front like she owned it as she did every place she walked into. She chuckled. With her newfound business, she could own it. She saw Harold's red Ferrari parked out front and knew he was home. She started to use her key, but decided to ring the bell. Juanita, the housekeeper, answered.

"Senorita Savage, I didn't know Senior Black was expecting you."

"He's not," Lexi responded, and then pushed her way past Juanita inside the house.

The look on Juanita's face told Lexi Harold had a bitch in the house, so she wanted to surprise him. She crept through the house, knowing there was only one place they would be. There was a room set up just for bitches. She went upstairs, stopped at the master bedroom and left her bags, then walked down the hall to the room she knew he was at. "Bingo," she whispered when she heard sounds of fucking. She could care less he was fucking someone else, she just wanted to catch him in the act to prove her point. She slowly opened the door and peeked in. Harold was spread out on the king sized bed getting his dick sucked by a light skinned bitch with a blond, white girl sitting on his face. *Just like Harold.* Lexi quietly crept in the room and sat in the chair placed in the corner. While she watched the threesome, she began playing with her pussy. Live sex shows always turned her on. After light bright got him rock hard from her head skills, she told snow bunny to slide on his dick while she rode his face. After snow bunny

came on Harold's dick, he told light bright to get on all fours so he could fuck her from behind. While doing so, she licked and sucked on snow bunny's pussy. Lexi wanted to join because she knew Harold's dick game was on point, but she didn't. The threesome was finally aware of her presence when she began moaning loudly from making herself cum.

The girls were oblivious, but Harold knew that voice, that moan, anywhere. He stopped what he was doing and looked toward the corner. "Lexi?" he said.

"The one and only," she replied.

"Damn, baby, why you ain't let me know you was coming?" he asked as he ignored the two horny girls and exited the bed.

"If I did, I would have missed the mind blowing show," she said, and then winked.

"You are something else, my queen."

The girls paid no mind to what was going on. They kissed and fondled each other.

"I'm here, so what's up?" Lexi asked.

"Let's go have a drink and talk."

She raised her brows and shrugged her shoulders. "Sounds good to me."

They went downstairs to the sitting room and Juanita made them a drink. "It's a nice night tonight."

"It is. Why don't we enjoy our drinks in the Jacuzzi?" That was Lexi's favorite place in the house. It was quiet and serene with green plants and flowing waterfalls, the opposite of what she had known her entire life.

"Anything for you, baby."

Lexi shot a smirkish smile and walked to the Jacuzzi when Juanita had delivered their drinks. When they got there she stripped naked and slid her body into the warm, bubbly water. There was an awkward silence that Lexi hadn't experienced before, and she thought it would be best to break it.

"Cut the bullshit, Harold. We ain't in none of them fairytale ass stories where everything ends up perfectly. We both came from fucked up lives, and this," she said, spreading her arms apart, "is what we know. We hustle, gaffle, grind, and get over. We do

whatever we need to in order to make our lives better." Harold looked like he was about to say something, but Lexi hushed him. "Look, I ain't knocking you for your hustle at all, and I expect you to not knock me for mine. What? You think we'll get married at the little white church, and have two point five kids with a perfect house that is surrounded with a white picket fence where we have a guard dog named Rocky? I don't even want kids, never wanted to be married, and damn sure don't like animals."

Harold moved closer to Lexi and put his arms around her. "That's what makes us perfect. I don't want that shit, either. I want to live the life I live, have a down ass bitch that don't expect me to be perfect, and won't flip out if I fuck another bitch. I want a bitch to understand what it feels like to love sex and be addicted to that shit, and someone that doesn't think monogamy and soul mates is the end all, be all. You're that bitch."

Lexi let out a chuckle. "You could be right, but nothing lasts forever. What am I supposed to do when you want to trade me in for the younger model? Do we get a prenup together where I make sure I'm taken care of for the rest of my life? Maybe you didn't notice, but I'm a hustla, too, and best believe Lexi Savage gonna be set till she fucking die. I don't need no fairytale bullshit, Harold. I don't need a dream that life could be different than I expected. All I want is what I expect. I got a lot of love for you and if you feel the same, we'll be friends forever. When you come to the Town I'll always make sure you feel like royalty, and when I come here I expect no less. Maybe one day we'll slow down and look into this marriage shit, but until then, let's ride it till the wheels fall off."

"Damn, you drive a hard bargain. I can respect where you coming from, so we'll make a toast to us." Harold raised his glass. He had hoped their meeting had gone another way, but like many before him, he knew when Lexi's mind was made, that was it. "Hustle over love."

Lexi raised her glass. "Till the wheels fall off." They drank and proceeded to fuck the shit out of each other the rest of the night.

Harold looked at her. "You know, even though your ID says you're twenty something, we couldn't officially get married

until you turned eighteen, anyways. Maybe by then you'll change your mind." It was the wee hours of the morning and they were hugged up in his enormous bed.

Lexi knew Harold knew, but he never let on. That could put him in a lot of trouble. "How long have you known?"

"Come on, queen, I've always known. I could have fucked myself up with still letting you film, but like you said, we're both hustlas."

The next morning, Lexi had her engagement ring replaced with a bigger one. "Friendships are more important than love, so they deserve a bigger ring. No matter what, I'll always love you."

"Whatever you say." Lexi looked at her ring and wondered if she would be Ms. Hope one day, tired of the hustle and ready for something secure. *Harold has money, but will that be secure? Would he be able to take care of me forever?*

Ms. Hope had some square ass nigga that knew nothing about the hustle. He probably had a nine to five that could barely afford one outfit she wore out of the month. He loved her, bought her roses and small trinkets, but it was nothing. She bought him thousand dollar gifts, took him on exotic vacations, and showed him a life he had only dreamed of. Lexi knew that would only last for so long, and she would be crawling back to the life she was used to living. Lexi knew how the game went, and that was why her workers met once a week and chill with each other. They shared stories, personal lives, and got to know each other. If she knew nothing else, she knew when niggas got to know each other on a personal level they wouldn't jump ship.

She spent two weeks with Harold and even did a few guest appearances at a couple of clubs while she was in LA, but it was time for her to get back home. Harold would visit her next when their schedules permitted.

Just as she suspected, when she got back from LA Bianca told her Ms. Hope called several times, trying to get in touch with her. When Lexi returned the call, Ms. Hope admitted that she thought she made a mistake and wanted to take her empire back over.

"Well, if your team wants you back, then they are all yours."

Lexi often got under minded because she was young. People didn't think she could handle business and keep her head straight being a seventeen year old girl. She loved the doubters because she always made them believers. When Ms. Hope came back and thought she was going to reclaim her clan, she got a rude awakening.

Everyone sat quiet with their heads down. They gave her respect and listened to what she had to say, but at the end of the day they weren't down for her anymore. They all knew Lexi well and knew she would speak for all of them.

When Ms. Hope was done, she met Lexi in her office and looked around. "Nice."

"Yea, it's how boss bitches do it."

"Look, you little bitch, I can give up names and crumble this whole operation. I can turn your lil' young ass in and get Harold in a lot of trouble for shooting movies with an underage girl. Bitches forget I made this shit," Ms. Hope said, reaching for needles in a haystack.

"Go ahead, boo. I've expanded further than you could ever touch. You gave it up and gave me the control, don't get mad because I did what you couldn't," Lexi said smoothly. "Oh, and Harold and After Dark Productions, take a shot, you will be shot down." The last thing Lexi ever wanted to do was get Harold in any kind of trouble, but she knew Ms. Hope wouldn't take it there.

"I will take your black ass down."

Lexi shrugged her shoulders and let out a girlish laugh. "In case you forgot, I'm a grown ass woman. I rule everything I touch." She extended her hand across the table and let her manicured nail stop just short of Ms. Hope's hand. "And, if I touch you again, I'll rule your old ass and have you on my payroll. We can do this however you want, but best believe I'll win." Lexi reached in her drawer and pulled out a nail file. She pretended to file her nails. "Take your old ass to that safe ass nigga that can keep you comfortable in outlet shit that may keep you just one notch above the bitches in your life right now. If you were smart, you saved enough money to maintain, if not, your loss. You want a war, you got one, boo boo."

Ms. Hope fumed. She didn't have strength for a war and she was pissed that Lexi read her like an open book. Her man's bank account was definitely smaller than hers and she got tired of taking care of him. He had no idea of her wild, sex filled life and he was so common. It took her forever to get him to be comfortable with toys in the bedroom. Ms. Hope thought it was cute at first, but not being able to let loose drove her crazy. She put in a porn that had a gangbang going on and her man lost it. She tried all girl porn and he was disgusted. He was happy with straight, one man, one woman sex. She was happy single and miserable married, but she did it to herself.

She let out a small laugh. "You're right, Sexi Lexi. I made my bed and I have to lie in it. Keep your head on straight and don't let some love bullshit take you off your game."

Ms. Hope smoothed her skirt, blew Lexi a kiss, and walked out of her office. Lexi finally exhaled. She didn't want to take it there with Ms. Hope because she still had a small bit of love for her, but she was prepared if she had to.

CHAPTER 20

"Lexi, I'm in love."

Lexi sat across from Bianca and kept a straight face. She knew her girl would die looking for love, and she kinda wanted her to find it. She had become the most normal, whatever normal was.

"If you're happy, then I'm happy for you, boo. Who is this dude?"

"Remember the one I mentioned a time or two, Rick?" Bianca knew Lexi was hella against love so she tried to contain her excitement from her. She wanted to be sure first, and she was.

"Oh yea, I remember the name."

"Well, he's met the family, including the kids. I'm really feeling him, and I think he's feeling me, too."

"What's his story?"

"He has twin boys with his high school sweetheart. They were supposed to get married, but she got cold feet and left him and the kids. He's really a nice guy. He has a job in the IT department at Children's Hospital."

"Does he know everything about you?"

"Yes. He's never judged me. He's been supportive and pushes me to be better."

"Are you going to leave me?"

"I love my job, Lex, you know that. I have flexible hours, the pay is great, and the medical is off the chain."

Lexi laughed. "I'm going to get a little emotional for a moment, so don't mind me. We've been friends a long time and I don't trust many muthafuckas, but I trust you with my life. I

couldn't imagine having anyone else as my right hand besides you. I'm in and out of a lot of shit, and I need to trust the person I put in charge to have my back. If this guy is who you want, really, I'm happy for you, but how do you know he's the one?"

"I feel it. I have my own now, I don't need a nigga paying bills or giving me money to maintain. We're on the same level." It was quiet for a while. "Look, Lex, you're my girl and this is the only reason Imma say this, Harold is your one. I've never seen two people more made for each other. When he's around, you glow, and for a bitch as dark as you, glowing is a special job," Bianca joked.

Lexi shook her head. "I don't have time to get caught up. That love shit is for the birds. You give up shit, you be who the person wants you to be, have a kid or two, then you're left high and dry, taking on responsibilities you aren't ready for. You get cold and bitter, and then you get old and lonely."

"Don't you see, Lex? You're already cold and bitter. You're so scared of love you won't give it a try. You've been raised and bred to be a cold hearted bitch, and you've taken that to heart." She reached across the desk and put her hand on top of Lexi's. "You deserve to be loved, too."

Lexi shook her head and rolled her eyes. "Harold is cool. I love chilling with him. But, love ain't shit. You get shitted on in love. He was leaving message after message about how he was in love and missed me, and when I popped up on his ass he was fucking two bitches. That's what niggas do, so it wasn't a letdown because I already expected it."

"That's what you guys do, so you know him fucking other bitches was nothing."

"It wasn't, but for a nigga to talk all that love shit, he sure didn't have a problem moving on. I got your back no matter what and I hope this nigga all you think he is, but while you chasing love, I'm chasing dollars."

"Dollars can't hold you at night and give you the security you crave."

Lexi laughed. "Shit, in my world, the almighty dollar rules every muthafucking thing. If it don't make dollars, it damn sure don't make sense."

"Harold makes dollars, plenty of them. You know that."

"I'm fucked up, he's fucked up, and together, nothing but fucked up bullshit will transpire. I'm a realist. How many people you thought would be together forever? How many people have you known that made you drop your jaw because they split? Love is overrated."

"You didn't think that when you loved Bank Roll."

Hearing his name made her heart stop. So many years had passed, but words could have never expressed the emptiness she felt from him being ripped from her life so soon. She knew she'd never love anyone like she loved him, and she didn't want to try. She knew everything she shared with him was the main reason she stayed as emotionless as she was. She had a lot of fun and a lot of great sex, but emotions weren't part of her master plan.

"You're right, I didn't think that. He was my one love in life and I'm cool with that."

"Don't you get tired of being lonely? Don't you want someone that has your back?"

Lexi laughed. "This sounds like a convo we had a few years ago. Bianca, I know you want love and I'm more than happy if you've found that. I want you to have more happiness than you can stand, and respect that right now I'm happy."

Bianca sighed. "I believe you, Lex. I guess we all have our own definition of happiness. Anyways, I'm having a que this weekend for Shaquanisha birthday."

"Damn, I forgot her birthday coming up. How old she about to be?"

"Girl, her lil' grown butt turning six. And, what kind of godmother are you that don't even know the kids' ages?"

"You know times flies in my life."

"You need to slow down every once in a while."

"I'll be there. So, is lover boy gonna be there?"

"Yes, that's why I really want you to come. Everybody's been asking about you. We just gonna chill out and enjoy life."

"Sounds good to me. Want me to bring anything?"

"Just you."

"I'll be there with bells on."

"I've invited the staff to come and I made sure no one had any dates set up for Saturday."

"So, you took it upon yourself to take money out of my pockets, huh?"

Bianca looked nervous. Her and Lexi was tight, but she knew Lexi was about business. "I'm sorry if I overstepped my bounds, I'll…"

Lexi laughed. "Damn, bitch, I'm fucking with you. I love it. We need to spend time together and let our hair down."

Saturday rolled around and Lexi was at Bianca's house bright and early to help out any way she could. She brought several bottles of alcohol along with cases of beer and Smirnoffs.

"Did you buy the whole store?" Bianca's mother asked when she opened the door.

"I just wanted to make sure there was enough. It's a kid's party, but you know how we do it."

"Hell yea. Let's get it popping." Tootie, Bianca's mother, had gone to rehab and vowed to stay clean of drugs. She still drank a few beers, maybe a shot of alcohol, but that was it.

"Baby, Lexi's here. I really want you to meet her," Bianca said to Rick, who was grilling meat. She pulled him from the grill and through the house. "Lexi!" she screamed as if she hadn't seen her in ages. She beamed all over, ready to show off her man.

Lexi put on the biggest smile possible. "Hey, girl. You looking good today." She turned her attention to Rick. "And, you must be the guy taking up all my girl's free time these days." She gave him a warm hug.

"I've heard so much about you, Lexi. It's good to finally meet you."

"Same here."

"Well, let's get this party started." Lexi popped a bottle of champagne and toasted to their love.

"I love you, girl."

"Auntie Lexi, what you get me for my birthday?"

"It's rude to ask for presents," Bianca scolded.

Lexi shook her head. "No, it's not, sweetie. Your birthday is your special day and anyone in your presence should have something for you." Shaquanisha looked at her mother and gave a

smirk as if to say, 'I told you so.' Lexi went in her huge purse and pulled out something. "Now that we talking about it, I think I got something special just for you." She gave the black, velvet box to Shaquanisha. She opened it to reveal a caret of diamond, teardrop earrings. Lexi stooped down to her level. "Diamonds and platinum are a girl's best friend, and let these diamond teardrops be the only ones you shed." Lexi gave her a big hug. "I love you."

"Thank you, Auntie Lexi, and I love you."

"We about to turn this party out." BJ walked over to hug Lexi. "Look at my lil' BJ getting all big. You almost tall as me now." He smiled and ran off. There was no party like a Bay party, no matter if it was for kids or adults, they partied like no other.

Lexi watched Bianca and her man. They both seemed really happy. Although Lexi knew it was wrong, she wanted to test him. She had gone to the bathroom and as if on cue, Rick happened to be passing when she opened the door. She grabbed him, backed him against the wall, and stuck her tongue down his throat. It took him about half a second to get it together and push Lexi away. She moved closer in his space.

"Don't play, you know you want it." She reached down and grabbed his dick.

Rick threw his hands up. "Look, Lexi, Bianca has always spoken highly of you and I don't know why you'd want to do something like this to her, but I can tell you I'd never betray her. I love her."

"Sure you do. I saw that look you gave me when you first saw me. You want it, don't you?"

Lexi was sexy, Rick couldn't deny that, but Bianca was who he loved. He had fucked up before by not being able to control his dick and he vowed he'd never let that happen again.

"You should be ashamed of yourself. How can you call yourself her friend? I love her so I won't tell her about this, but I suggest you keep your hands to yourself from now on."

Lexi smiled. "Either you knew this was a test or you really love my girl. I'm going to hope it's the latter and wish you guys nothing but happiness."

Rick exhaled. "Lexi, I do love her. My heart was pounding because I really thought you were trying to come onto me and I felt bad for Bianca. She loves you."

"I know it was a dirty move, but I want her to be happy. Everybody knows men hardly ever think with the right head."

"Been there before, but I'm older and wiser now."

"Good. Do her right or I'll fuck you up."

Cherry walked over to Lexi when she saw her come out of the house. "Hey, Lexi, what's good?"

"Same ole same. What's up with you? I'm glad you came out to Sha's birthday party."

"You know I can't turn down a good party. I like how you keep our money right, but you make us feel like family."

Lexi shrugged. "I know most of us are lost souls with no family, gotta start somewhere."

"You right about that."

"What you doing later, wanna chill with me?"

"Absolutely."

Lexi told her workers they couldn't be involved with each other, but that didn't stop her from chilling with Cherry. They had started their lust for each other way before Fantasies and no one would come between that.

After Shaquanisha opened her gifts and they cut the cake, people began to go their separate ways. Lexi gave Bianca and Rick a hug, and told them she would get up with them later. She passed Bianca's mom on the way out and listened to one of her wild stories before finally leaving. When Lexi pulled up to her home, Cherry was already waiting outside. Lexi unlocked the door and led Cherry inside.

"I'll go start the water."

Cherry knew Lexi loved to be clean before any sexual act. She filled the large, Jacuzzi tub with warm water and bubbles. She lit a few candles and started slow music. She loved chilling with Lexi, she always made her feel loved.

They sank in the bubbles. "Why won't you fuck with Harold?"

"You know how love works. You think it's cool when it's really not."

"He loves you, I can tell, and I know you love him."

"Love ain't always enough. Did you come over here to fight his battle?"

"No, I just never met anyone like you. Most women spend their whole life looking for love, and I think you'll spend your whole life running from it."

"When did you first fuck a woman?" They had talked about so much, but never that.

"I was about fifteen. That nigga my momma was fucking with had gone to jail and I went home 'cause I ain't have nowhere else to go. She was some chick that sold to my momma. She was a butch, though, not really my cup of tea. She dressed and acted like a dude. One day, my momma wanted to get high and didn't have no money. Tone said she would let my momma get high if she could taste my pussy. My momma, her ass ain't hesitate to send me with Tone.

"That shit was crazy. She took me to a room, a fancy one, and she gave me flowers and shit. She filled the tub with water and washed my body. She was really tentative. It was weird because I didn't know what to expect, but she took me to the bed, laid me down, and the rest was history. She was a butch, but when she took her clothes off she was all woman. She had a nice shape and kept her pussy shaved. Her touch was so soft and I loved it. We kissed all night and sucked each other's pussy. I fucked with her for a while after that."

"Do you like men or women more?"

"I don't know. I like 'em both."

"I feel you, me too. I asked myself hella times what I liked more. Ms. Hope ass turned me out. I really do think I loved her way more than Bank Roll, but there's something about a hard, pulsating dick inside of me."

"I agree with you there. It's a trip how crazy sex shit from being young makes you turn to crazy sex shit when you're older."

"Guess 'cause it's all we know. Imagine all of us on an episode of Oprah." Cherry laughed and Lexi joined. "What you think about that Rick dude?" Lexi was firm on her decision that he was good peeps, but she wanted to hear what Cherry thought without swaying her opinion.

165

"I think he cool. The whole time, he didn't look at anyone. There weren't any lustful, uncomfortable stares. Men look, that's a given, but he always kept his eyes on her and showed her and the kids a lot of love."

Lexi smiled. "I know it's fucked up, but I tried that nigga. I was all on his ass and he basically pushed me off and told me I was a fucked up friend."

Cherry shrugged. "If he was able to push you away, he love her ass."

They sipped Grey Goose as they chatted. Finally, they got out of the tub and walked over to Lexi's bed. Cherry was a pain freak, so Lexi grabbed one of the candles and slowly poured the wax on her. Cherry moaned and wiggled. When the wax dried, Lexi lightly licked the burned spots. She bit Cherry's nipples and pinched her clit. She grabbed the nipple clamps from her nightstand and put them on Cherry.

"Turn over in the doggie position." Cherry turned over, and Lexi began eating her pussy while she slightly pulled on the clamps every now and again. Lexi turned her over and kissed her. She opened her nightstand again and pulled out the strap on. She grabbed a handful of Cherry's hair. "Suck it." Cherry licked her lips and sucked the plastic dick with conviction. Sometimes, Lexi wondered how it would feel to have a real dick. She wanted to get hard and watch a bitch slurp on her dick until she came. Lexi gripped tighter on Cherry's hair and forced the dick down her throat, almost making her throw up. Cherry loved it, and her pussy swelled. "That's right, get that dick real wet."

After a few more minutes, Lexi pushed Cherry back on the bed. She opened her legs and forced the dick inside of her, fucking her hard. She bent her legs back and fucked her pussy while she kissed her. Cherry held on tight as she thrust her hips to meet Lexi's strokes. She loved Lexi, but she would never tell her that because she knew how she was. Lexi stopped kissing her and flipped her over. She spat in Cherry's ass and shoved the dick inside and fucked her until she made Cherry cum.

"Come suck this dick and finger my pussy."

Cherry did as told, sucking the dick while she had her fingers buried in Lexi's pussy. She used her thumb to rub her clit

and it didn't take long before Lexi came hard. Then, Cherry put on the strap on and fucked Lexi. They fucked each other until they passed out.

CHAPTER 21

A few years had gone by. Unique and Tasty had left the organization. Lexi had a top paying client that wanted to be with a man and a woman and even though Unique said she was down, when she witnessed the men fucking she couldn't stomach it and left. Tasty met some dude she was feeling and wanted to leave that lifestyle alone to be with him. Lexi was irritated, but she let them go. Chicks like them were a dime a dozen. A couple of the men had come and gone, but they were easily replaceable.

Bianca was ready to be a full time housewife. She would never up and leave Lexi, so she waited until she could find someone to help her. Lexi thought of Cherry, but she knew her head wasn't in the right place. She was in love and Lexi knew it, and if she gave her a power position like being her assistant Cherry could fuck it all up if she felt scorned. She figured she'd hit up a club she worked back in the day and see if they had any fresh meat for her to recruit.

As she sat in a dark corner and drank shots of Patron with Bud Light Lime, she was surprised to see her cousin on stage working it. They hadn't seen each other in years, but she knew her family. She watched how her cousin worked the crowd, and how almost every nigga threw dollars at her left and right. *Hmm, destiny is a muthafucka.* She knew she bumped into her cousin at exactly the right time.

"Damn, I ain't seen you in forever," Drama said to Lexi when she saw her sitting at a private table in T&A. She gave her a

hug. "Damn, cousin, you looking good. What the fuck you been up to?"

"I'm surviving. I came in here to check some shit out. I got a lil' business and I think you would fit in perfectly. What time you get off?"

"I got one more set to do and I'm outta here. Damn, Lexi, you just what I need right now."

"You have no idea." Lexi ordered another drink and watched her cousin handle her business. As she watched, she knew Drama would be a good fit. She was comfortable in her body and comfortable making money. "Let's go grab some breakfast and talk," Lexi said, and then followed Drama out of the club.

Drama caught Lexi up on family drama and Lexi told her a little bit about what she was into. She was glad to hear that Yesina had been around. For them to be sisters, they didn't know shit about each other and hadn't seen each other in years. She always meant to call or drop by, but her schedule was too busy.

Drama followed up with a visit to the office the next day, and when it was said and done Lexi knew she would be a perfect fit for Rico and John, the trick that wanted to be with a man and woman. Lexi had made the run a couple of times before, but she was about business, she wasn't really into fucking the clients.

Not more than a month had passed and since Lexi didn't tell Drama her rule of the workers not fucking with each other, she couldn't be mad when her cousin got caught up with Rico. He knew the rule, but Lexi figured it had to be something special because Rico never crossed the line. She decided to let them do their thang and if anyone else had something to say, she'd deal with it. It was a new day for Lexi and Fantasies, and as she had lived her life from the beginning, she was gonna ride the shit till the wheels fell off.

Harold was in town and Lexi planned on spending the evening with him. It was Valentine's day and although she was against it, she was going to act like they were a couple in love for lover's day and enjoy the moment. They went to Yoshi's and were serenaded by Maxwell crooning seductive hits. They danced and laughed. They had made an effort to spend more time together and

although Lexi wanted to fight it, she couldn't. She loved Harold and everything he stood for, and she had given his proposition of them being together more thought. He didn't pressure, but he always let it be known that he was in love and that wasn't going to change.

Once the song was over, they sat at their table. "Let's toast, queen," Harold suggested.

"To what?" Lexi asked as she lifted her glass."

"As always, to friendship. I love you, Lexi."

Lexi smiled. After years, she finally felt it was time. "Harold, I lo..." She had stopped mid sentence at the sight before her. She put down her glass and was speechless.

Harold was on the edge of his seat. "Queen, are you OK?"

Lexi didn't respond. She rubbed her eyes and looked again in the same direction that had caught her attention. Tears filled her eyes, but not a drop slid down her face. "It can't be," she whispered to herself.

"Baby, you're scaring me."

Without saying anything, Lexi got up from her seat and walked across the room. She stood in front of him and knew her eyes hadn't been deceiving her.

He looked up and admired the red Herve Leger dress that hugged her curvaceous body. The Manolos that graced her pedicured feet were gorgeous. Her makeup was flawless and her hair was soft and sexy. What made his heart skip a beat was when he looked in those hypnotizing eyes and saw them filled with water.

"Baby girl, it's been a long time."

Lightning Source UK Ltd.
Milton Keynes UK
UKOW041859070712

195630UK00005B/67/P